IMPOSTOR FIGURES

I. D. FILIP

In memory of mom.

For being the woman nobody knew you were.

To all women.

Fighting their inner fight to be what the world

wants them to be.

PROLOGUE

I'm an impostor. I wrote a book in a language that's not mine, about five women that aren't me. And yet, I must confess: parts of them are me. Perhaps there are parts of every woman out there. What started as a creative expression in time turned into an act of self-redemption. You may disagree with it or you may find yourself in it. What I ask of you, as you begin with the first page, is to accept it. With all its flaws. Even when it disagrees with your beliefs, norms, or values. Accept it. Even when the language feels different, when the words become too heavy, when it gets dark. Accept it. Before we truly can accept who we are, we have to accept what is it that makes us different.

I'm an impostor, learning to be myself every day.

"We are all born pure.
Then we become impostors."

ONS

Chapter 1

Vee

When Vee was around 13 years old in the early '90s and started discovering her mom's makeup and reading about low-fat diets, spinning classes, and pencil-thin eyebrows in women's magazines, she was a pretty typical adolescent, filled with insecurity, crimped hair, and too much eyeliner. She also quickly was becoming one of the leading bullies in school, seeking desperate attention from her friends and praise for her beauty from the boys she liked and even the ones she didn't. She was ready to take on the world, do ballet, or even model, as well as marry well and move to the big city under bright lights. With a bit of luck, the odds were in her favor for her to achieve all of this – but the odds have their own way of fulfilling a destiny.

Call it odds, call it destiny, but it was on one of these days that a car crashed into her, dragged her for 49 feet, and ran her over when her shirt got caught on the car's bumper. Ran over her dreams, beliefs, and what she thought she'd become. To this day, when people hear this story from Vee, they only know half of it. They don't know that she couldn't actually feel the impact of the car hitting her tiny hips, the blood pouring from her limbs, her head smashing on the ground, or her flesh dragged on the hot asphalt on that summer day. They don't know that it wasn't the impact that was the most painful, but rather going through puberty and adolescence living with the scars the crash left behind. A split second was all it took for her destiny to change forever. If you knew Vee before the accident, you'd understand why.

After Vee awakened on the ground, disoriented and confused, an unknown man suddenly picked her up and carried her to his car, put her in the back seat, and drove away. She then started to grasp that something was terribly wrong. "Am I being kidnapped?" she thought, perhaps even mumbling, "Help!" with whatever strength she had left in her body. Her mom taught her well to avoid strangers, and she was ready to fight back and follow her mom's advice. However, this man came out of nowhere, and she just didn't have time to fight back. He was as fast as the Tasmanian Devil from the Looney Tunes cartoons she loved so much, so it took her a few minutes to realize that he wasn't kidnapping her, but actually saving her life. To this day, she still can remember the smell of leather, cigarettes, and gasoline inside his car. The back window was a little cracked, and the mid-June sun's rays awakened her from her dizziness. She sat up, looked down at her legs, and saw tire tread marks on her right calf, carved into her flesh, leaving traces of melted rubber. She was numb, and this certainly wasn't a kidnapping, though now she kind of wished it were. She was hit by a car and was being rushed to the emergency room.

She felt nothing but fear and confusion, with the trauma blocking all the pain. Blood was pouring from her limbs onto her unicorn white shirt, flowered sneakers, and the filthy carpet of this old car, yet all she could think about was – *"Damn it, not the sneakers."*

Two days later, she was in a coma. Four days later she survived death. Four months later, she was able to walk again. Four years later, she began hiding her scars from her first date. Decades later, she still was hiding them.

On this particular day we're about to go through, almost 16 years later, Vee was sitting on a chaise lounge in front of Carlton during a scorching heat wave. Sweat was dripping down her forehead, making her sunglasses slide down her thin nose, and she was daydreaming about diving into the cold Mediterranean water about 50 feet in front of her. But she wasn't ready to take the plunge. There were too many people around, and she didn't want the attention that she would've wanted back in 1994. This time around, too many eyes were staring at her without anybody actually looking in her direction. Moreover, nobody knew the fight going on inside of her, so to everybody around her, she looked like everyone else. For that matter, considering her age and the career she had begun to build for herself, some would say that "she made it."

Vee chose which people she wanted to know her carefully. She had become an expert at bending realities by the time she reached middle school. When other girls were dealing with puberty – hating that their breasts were too small, their hair was too short, they weren't tall or skinny enough, they didn't have blue eyes, or they had too many pimples – all Vee wanted was not to have the scars on her leg, arm, and back from the accident. That's all she wanted. However, puberty is hard on people, so she played along and voiced the common complaints and swallowed the ones that truly mattered to her. She, too, had to be vocal about hating her curly hair, height, small breasts, big calves, and not having her mom's gorgeous green eyes. Of course, all these were lies. She couldn't care less about all of the above. She would've traded anything not to have those scars, but puberty was tough on her, so she had to fight back the best way she could – by hiding from the truth.

Vee refused to wear skirts or T-shirts. To fight back questions such as "Aren't you hot?" in 90-degree weather while wearing jeans, she fabricated a characteristic about herself that soon everyone accepted – cold intolerance. Thus, when someone asked her that question, she replied, *"I'm always cold. I'm weird that way,"* even as sweat dripped beneath her top, her legs were melting in her tight jeans, and her hair was curling up from the humidity. And this was just late June, but she just learned to live like that. Perhaps that's why she hates saunas.

Every time she went on a first date, she wondered when her date would discover her scars. The scar on her hand was easy to excuse, as it wasn't very ugly, or big, and it served as the perfect decoy. She usually pretended that the scar was *"nothing really"* and went along with the idea that it looked like she had burned her hand, when in fact it was way more than that. When she disclosed that it was from a car accident, their usual question was *"Oh my god, were you driving?"* then she always made the same weird joke: *"Yes, I was 12."* She then waited for a second to let that information sink in with her audience, then through a classic smoke screen, she calmed everything down with reassurance: *"Just kidding. I was hit by a car when I was a kid. It was a long time ago. I can hardly remember."* And just like that, the conversation would end there, maybe because people, more often than not, wondered why she made a stupid joke, or maybe because they were still processing it. But it worked. She never left the conversation open-ended, and you really could never ask more than that. She didn't want to lie about how many scars she had, or what happened, so she just learned to avoid the conversation and lead people into believing that a small scar on her hand was the only scar. After all, we all have scars, don't we?

But it always was nerve-racking – enduring summer heat, feeding new boyfriends a pack of lies about why she wouldn't wear skirts, saying she was cold all the time even if she wasn't. She had lived for two decades under this painful routine of deceit, dreading summer, when she had to pretend she doesn't like to play volleyball on the beach, or that she's on her period when she went to pool parties. Two decades of choosing the lesser of two evils – when she thought looking weird was better than looking like a freak.

Now let's talk about sex for a minute. She had sex for the first time when she was 17, gracefully dodging the challenge of who's going to lose her virginity first among her high school friends. Not because she wasn't offered it or because she wanted to ignore it, but because she wasn't brave enough not to. She was the last one of her friends to have sex because she was too stressed about the world finding out what she really looked like. However, as she suspected when she decided to push it back a few more years, sex would become a nerve-racking experience too. She began masturbating at a young age, so she kind of knew how things worked down there. It wasn't the idea of sex itself that terrified her – it was the thought of a boy seeing her completely naked, that someone would see her as she really was.

Yet somehow, she learned how to master the coverup during sex too. Sex from behind? Yes, she could hide her leg under the covers. Sex with feet up in the air? Perfect. The scar was on the outer part of her right leg, so in the midst of it all, he wouldn't see it. Sex lying on her side? Even better. It's always going to be on the right side, so she'll make something up for the other one. Oral sex? Yes. Both ways. She had developed her own *Kama Sutra* rules – defined not by pleasure, but by the scars that defined her. Pleasure was something she learned to master under strict rules – her own rules – and somehow that made it more desirable. She became promiscuous, and for many years, she chose the swipe-left kind of get-together rather than a relationship with too many details about her life.

Don't get too involved – he'll see it. Don't get too close – he'll break your heart. Don't stay too long – he'll soon find out you're not like the rest of the world. So, in an effort to convince herself that she's just like everyone else, she started going to the gym long before most people do. She became addicted to how her abs looked, how her arms looked, how toned she was. She wanted to attract men using areas of her body that remained untouched by her past.

As she was sitting on the chaise lounge in front of Carlton, she closed her eyes, took a deep breath, and got up.

"I'm gonna do it," she thought to herself and suddenly ran toward the sea.

The burning sand that would make anyone run fast toward the cold water was the perfect alibi.

"Are you going in?" her best friend Chloe yelled after her, barely catching a glimpse of Vee running away toward the water.

"YES! Come on, Chloe, the sand is burning," Vee screamed back without looking behind or stopping.

"Woman! Why didn't you tell me you're going for a dip? I'm coming," Chloe mumbled back, realizing there's no point in yelling after her. Vee was already gone.

Vee was already close to the shore, and as she approached the water, where a lot of people were just sitting there people-watching and getting a tan, like a marathon runner, she pushed her speed limit right before the finish line, then made the split-second decision to jump into the cold water, make a splash, and blur the audience's view. The sooner she could get her feet underwater, the less likely anyone would stare at her. Years and years of practicing beach exposure strategy were paying off on that beach in St. Tropez.

"Woo hoo!" she screamed with delight, as she finally managed to take that sweat off her heated body.

"You're crazy! It's too cold," Chloe screamed from the shore, barely placing her feet in the water.

Finally relaxed and camouflaged by the Mediterranean, Vee started to jump up and down, playing with her toes inside the sand underwater. She looked at her feet distorted by the water and the sun's rays, and finally felt free. She threw herself on her back in the cold water and was just lying there, afloat, enjoying the sun's rays and the calmness of the peaceful waves lifting her weight up and down, like a perfectly timed clock. The calm of being free, not judged, at most admired for her gracious swimming skills and perfectly shaped abs. It was the kind of calm that was rare, the lack of pressure she only felt in moments like this – staying afloat, still, on the salty water, enjoying the hot rays of a summer sun in the South of France.

"Aaaaaaa! Cold, cold, cold!" Chloe screamed as she got in and swam toward Vee, disrupting her moment of Zen.

"You're overreacting, Chloe."

Vee placed her feet back into the underwater sand and started swimming away from Chloe.

"Hey! Where are you going?" Chloe screamed.

"Away from you, crazy woman!" Vee replied, laughing.

A few meters out swimming, she noticed him staring at her and smiling.

"It's actually quite cold," he insisted.

"Right? Thank you!" Chloe approved from a distance. "This one here just has a different body temperature."

"I agree! She's pretty hot," he added.

Vee rolled her eyes and looked ironically at Chloe. They didn't need a secret nonverbal agreement to figure out his line was lame, so Chloe just burst into laughter.

"It's cheesy as fuck, but I, for one, can't say no to a good pun."

Vee shook her head in disapproval and continued swimming while smiling at the gorgeous man looking at her. He was the perfect prey for a Vee escape in St.Tropez, and she was now just analyzing him for what could be a pretty memorable sexual escapade.

"Coooome onnnnn," Chloe insisted. "Out of all the people on this beach, you gotta appreciate a good pun – aren't you a copywriter?"

"Used to be," Vee insisted, smiling.

Chloe let it go.

The guy was good-looking, tall, and fit, wearing a Patek Philippe watch on his wrist and looking as if he had no care in the world. He had that *"je m'en fiche"* kind of attitude that rich kids have. Surely that expression must have been coined on an expensive boat somewhere in the South of France. He could have been Swedish, German, or just a very white guy from California with a poignant *"fuck-me money"* accent, but he had style, so Vee was sold. He was the typical bachelor spending the summer in the South of France and the perfect match for Vee. No commitment, no life-sharing moments, no strings attached, so if he ever got to know her secret, who cared anyway? She was 1,000 miles away from home and not even imposture travels so fast or so far. *This* was freedom.

"I'm Frederick, but you can call me Freddie," he hollered at Vee, forcing an introduction.

"Hi, Freddie. I'm actually cold now," Vee quickly replied, playing her overestimated hard-to-get game. To him, it seemed that she was just swimming close to him, but she was already two steps ahead, swimming on his right side so she could strategize her return back to her sun bed. After all, Freddie now was watching her. Certainly, he'd want to ensure that she checks all the boxes before his second attempt, but Vee was like a Tetris expert on the beach. Years of practice on how to camouflage while navigating the beach in a swimming suit helped her assess the landscape and react quickly so that neither Freddie nor Chloe would notice anything out of the ordinary about her, or her *awkward* return to the sun bed. And just like that, she was off, running back to her sun bed.

"So, Freddie, huh?" Chloe asked rhetorically as she collapsed on the soft cushion.

"I mean – why not?" Vee added.

Her body had now cooled down, and her heart no longer was racing. Nobody saw the scars or asked her what happened. She could relax. She closed her eyes and listened to the sound of the ocean – breathe in, breathe out – and practiced her daily meditation minute to reconnect with her body. She read somewhere that if you reconnect with your body, you'll learn to love it more, and for a while now, it was working. She kept repeating in her mind: "You're strong, you're beautiful, you're healthy. You're strong, you're beautiful you're healthy. You're strong, you're beautiful, you're…"

"Your sunglasses are pretty dope," Freddie noted, interrupting her meditation.

Vee opened her eyes and smiled at him. She barely heard his voice the first time, but she just knew it was him. His style matched perfectly with an attitude in which he had to make no effort in his life to score. Granted, she understood exactly why and on that beach, in that moment in time, that all she wanted was what Freddie wanted – good sex.

"Who makes them?" he continued.

"What?"

"The glasses."

"Oh. Thom Yorke."

"Thom Yorke. They're from New York, aren't they?"

"Yes, I think so."

"I think they have a small shop in Williamsburg."

"Are you from New York?" Vee was surprised.

"Do I sound like I'm from New York?" Freddie laughed. "Where are you guys from?"

"Umm, from all over the world, to be honest – Boston, Seattle, these guys are from London, the other two are from San Diego, and that tall annoying one you just met, Chloe, she's from Paris," pointing at a big group on the beach.

"Quite the international crew. How do you know each other?"

"MBA."

"Nice. What do you do?"

"Advertising. What about you?"

"Commercial trade."

"What does that mean?"

"I help move things around the world – or around the bar. Wanna grab a drink?"

"Sure. I think you need some help with your pickup lines."

Freddie laughed and walked toward the bar: "See you in a bit."

Vee smiled and accepted his offer, but all she could think about was the strategy to hide her scars. The man just wanted to have fun, and so did she, so she wouldn't let something like old scars ruin an evening in St. Tropez. She always carried around one or two beach dresses with her, just in case opportunities like this arose, and she wanted to look the part. To an outsider, she may have sounded like a total nut job, but when you've conditioned your mind to think you're not good-looking enough for your entire life, it's hard to let go of that thought process as a 28-year-old. It had become a survival instinct.

She grabbed her straw bag and headed to the changing rooms. She pulled out a beautiful, long, wavy, floral dress, perfect for the South of France. She tried it on and checked herself in the mirror. It looked stunning, but she wondered whether Freddie would think it's a fake Dolce and that would put him off, so she pulled out the other one – a dark-green cami slip midi dress with sequin embellishment – the perfect trick for a night out, but was it right for the end of a day at the beach? Well, as with most things in life, Vee picked the lesser of two evils and went for the green dress – it covered all parts that needed to be covered, showed all the parts that needed to be shown, and screamed just the right amount of luxe to convert this guy into a believer.

As she approached the bar, Freddie was already on fire – he knew everyone serving drinks and was laughing with another bro from the Patek Philippe fan club.

"Hey!" Vee interrupted.

"Hey, you!" Freddie greeted her, probably having already forgotten her name.

"Man, this is my friend from New York!" he introduced Vee to his friend, confirming he had no idea what her name was.

"I'm Vee, and I'm actually from Boston." Vee then extended her arm for a handshake.

Freddie looked at her a bit disappointed, just like a European who likes to brag about their friends from New York or a New Yorker who likes to brag about their friends from Europe.

"You are?"

"Boston baby. Born and raised."

"I love Boston," his Patek Philippe bro added. "Well, actually Cape Cod."

Freddie started to laugh and high-fived him.

"Do you have a house in Cape Cod?" Freddie asked.

"My parents used to."

"Zuper," said Freddie with his German accent.

"Cute watch," his Patek bro added, pointing at her small-diameter Rolex as he walked away without saying goodbye. Granted, it was the smallest size a Rolex comes in, but she had worked hard to buy that $6,000 watch she always wanted, and "cute" wasn't really cutting it for her. She was 28! But when you sit in front of yacht boys wearing $100,000 gold watches on a beach, there's no point in feeding your ego, so Vee just smiled and waved.

Just an hour later, Freddie and Vee already had downed two mezcals, straight, so their minds started to slip toward what's next. Clearly, none of them wanted that date to be more than a fun night in St.Tropez. Vee was already used to this. A part of her was saying that this is right; it's better than giving explanations. A part of her was tired, needing someone to acknowledge her – not her smarts, humor, or success – but her beauty, someone with whom she could wake up in the morning, with him leaning over her, gazing into her sleepy eyes, under the morning sun, caressing her hair and telling her, "you're beautiful." That's all she wanted, but that's something girls experience only in romantic movies from Hollywood. Why is it that it's always the ugly, boring guys who say, "You're beautiful"? They must take the most desperate measures to get what they want. It's never the nice guys, the good ones, the ones that say you'll talk later and you actually do. Those guys never tell you, "You're beautiful." They tell you that you look nice, that you have nice shoes, that you're nice, that everything's nice – but nothing's ever beautiful.

Vee was sipping her mezcal sour, cleaning the salt off the rim of the glass, then licking it. It wasn't the sexual kind of licking, but the "I genuinely love this salt" kind of licking. Suddenly, Freddie put his hand on her leg and pushed her dress up close to her hips with what she had imagined was a sensual move. She leaned toward him and kissed him. It wasn't the romantic kind of kiss you see in movies at the beach bar when they finally realize they were made for one another, but rather the real-world kind of kiss – two drunk people at a bar in St.Tropez being part-sexy, part-sleazy. As they kissed, he moved his hand up her body and touched her breast. "Is this guy serious?" Vee thought to herself and gently leaned away from him.

"Excuse me for a minute," Vee said as she got up to head to the bathroom as Freddie watched her, surprised. Was that an invitation or was it a rejection?

As she walked toward the bathroom, a separate little hut on the beach, and distanced herself from the bar and the music, she could hear the sea again. She was quite dizzy from the drinks, and as she looked up at the stars dancing in the sky, she took a deep breath and stopped to just stand still for a minute. She loved staring at the sky. It always brought her peace. It was the quiet, calm vastness that anchored her into just how small and fragile we *all* are. Every once in a while, she could hear some glasses and plates clinking from the kitchen behind the bar. It seemed like the place slowly was shutting down, and it was just about time for her and Freddie to leave. A glass suddenly broke in the distance, bringing her back to the beach, almost as a cue that it was time for her to hit the bathroom and head back to leave.

She looked in the mirror at herself – surprisingly, her makeup was still good, a nice touch as her hair had curled up from the sea salt and humidity, and looked nothing like a few hours ago. She placed some lipstick on her salted lips and pressed her hands beneath her curly hair to give her a little pick-me-up.

Suddenly, she felt two hands on her waist and Freddie's cologne inundating the hut. He kissed her on the neck gently and pulled her hair away from her shoulders. His hands started to move from her waist down to her hips and slowly down to her legs. Clearly, Freddie thought it was an invitation. As his hands reached her knees, Vee instinctively pushed her bottom behind into his white linen pants and themselves into one of the stalls. They both smiled at each other as his hands suddenly went up her hips again, dragging along her long dress and revealing her black swimwear. He kissed her again on the neck as Vee moaned with pleasure, letting herself go under the starry sky, in a stall with dim light, on a beach in St. Tropez.

"You're beautiful when you moan like that," he said as he lowered his pants.

To Vee, *this* was freedom.

***

When she met David after many broken relationships, Vee felt reassured. It felt like he was in it for the long haul, but now the long haul seemed to be a marathon she might not be able to finish. Thoughts of their future started to crawl in, and slowly, that future turned into doubts. What would happen if they got married or had kids? Would he find out about her scars then? Should she tell him now? Will he feel betrayed, or should he have noticed by himself if he really cared in the first place? And what about when she has kids? What if he wants to be in the delivery room? What if her kid sees them – and 100% *will* – so then what's worse? Him knowing about it or him finding out? "Can you hear yourself?" She wondered many times. "If people heard what you think, they'd lock you up." As crazy as it sounded, trauma was so rooted that for a long time, Vee thought that nothing was strange about the idea that her future husband may not find out about her scars until she's on her death bed in old age. It made her therapist lose it every time she heard it, but Vee never wanted to hear about it. She had her way of closing down conversations and building invisible walls nobody could climb. When she did that, it didn't matter whether you were her therapist, best friend, nemesis, or husband. It's just how she operated.

However, while Vee sheltered in place behind her invisible wall, life happened. She and David moved in together, got married, lived in several houses, had been together for seven years, and he still didn't know about all her scars and hadn't seen them all. She still didn't have the courage to tell him about them, even though he wasn't a shallow man. He loved her, respected her, trusted her, yet Vee still kept thinking, *"What if he were repulsed by them? Would he want to be with a crippled woman, with someone different?"* After all, he never told her she was beautiful.

Vee was a professional impostor as an advertising professional. Day in and day out, she imagined people's lives and wrote idealistic stories that would persuade people into buying what they don't need. But living in an ad world also made her understand that body positivity still was a dream, a nice-to-have for the woke generation. The reality was that to this day, if she walked into a room and vouched for an actress with scars to play in one of her commercials for detergents, the client would freak out. They barely had begun accepting tattoos on actors' hands in recent years and finally came to terms with the idea of moms having tattoos too and that they're not all punks.

She knew that body positivity in culture was a myth, something you share on social media to get a "like." The world doesn't embrace it. They say they do, but really, they don't. She had to come to terms with the fact that so far, it seemed like you can't change cultural DNA – years of programming our collective brains on what beauty standards should be. And men like David wouldn't stand by her if she wasn't that – a beauty standard.

If he only knew what was happening inside her head – if only she could tell him and share this information with someone besides her therapist. It always felt like a skeleton inside her high-end, beautifully designed closet that few would have the courage to let out.

David wasn't the first man she ever lived with, and it wasn't the first time she lived with someone while hiding the scars from them, but just like with past relationships, after a while, she hoped David would notice her scars and say something. She wanted to be discovered so that she could lift the veil from her soul – the way some serial killers want to be discovered.

She read studies that reported jarring statistics supporting the idea that physical trauma may leave long-lasting effects on a person, and that those who go through it sometimes can develop into psychopaths. But she wasn't a psychopath – or was she?

Freud believed that people develop three aspects of their personality in early life – the id, the ego, and the superego.*1 The ego is formed as sort of a guide to remain aligned with societal norms. According to Freud's psychodynamic theory on serial killers, they have weak egos. Now, Vee had been brought up with a poor ego, and puberty and adolescence were shrouded in secrets concerning how she looked. Like any childhood trauma, talking about it wasn't easy, but this kind of trauma, though under the rug, wasn't

---

1(Seltzer 1995)

the kind that would go unnoticed forever. Quite the contrary, it was hiding in plain sight.

With Vee hiding her scars, the usual romantic days of the early relationship period weren't quite traditionally romantic. His T-shirt on her naked body was sexy, but she didn't have the legs of a model so that she could just walk around. When they snuggled, she'd always be on his left side so that she could roll over and put her left foot over him. When showering together, she'd stay close to him, kiss him, and not let his eyes look down. She was never hot, never wore skirts in summer, biked with long pants, and wore jeans at the beach quite often. David never got it and always commented on it.

At times, she became like a serial killer wanting to be caught. After years of hiding it, though exciting at the beginning of every relationship, it became tiring. She became more sloppy around the house about hiding the scars, more careless, but every time she had a moment of sanity, she'd hide them.

David was a Wall Street guy, so for him, relationships were everything. It takes knowing the right people, surrounding yourself with those who can help you be successful in life – that's what he believed. He built his reputation from the ground up without having any knowledge in finance, but he ran with the right crowds in New York. It was in one of those right crowds where Vee and him met. A few years later, they were married.

***

It was summertime, and it was crazy hot. After months and months of cold weather and clouds lurking over Manhattan, people were finally out and about, enjoying the sun, and rooftop party season slowly began.

Vee already was late from work for David's future partner dinner. He had asked her to join him for dinner with his potential new partner and his wife. She had known about this for a while, but was stuck at a pitch rehearsal. In the ad world, a pitch was the main protagonist of a future divorce. However, David never seemed to mind Vee's work schedule and actually appeared to be proud of it.

"I'm hoooome! Sorrrrrryyyyyy! I'll take a quick shower, and we can get the hell out of here."

Vee dropped her bag on the floor, threw her shoes in the closet, and without even going to check on David, took off her clothes and walked straight into the shower, leaving all the work traces behind on the floor.

"Hey," David walked in the bathroom after her.

"Hey, honey, I'm so sorry," replied Vee from behind the curtain.

"Don't worry about it; we still have time," he calmly reassured her.

Vee turned toward David and pushed the shower curtain away to take a look at her husband. He already was dressed up and looked gorgeous as he always did, wearing a black shirt tucked into his dark-gray pants with a black tie. She remembered why she married him in the first place, but also realized how lucky she was that he said yes to her.

"You look nice, baby," said Vee as she leaned in to kiss him.

"Careful, you're wet." He took a step back.

"Aren't you going to be hot in a suit?" she wondered.

"Look who's talking." He laughed. "The sun will set soon, so I'll be fine. It gets colder in the evening. Hurry up, I got you something."

"What? What? Whaaaatttt?" Vee screamed from behind the curtain with excitement as he stepped out, smiling, having anticipated she'd react like this.

David started to laugh as he knew that Vee couldn't stand surprises. She was too curious by nature to stand the pressure of a surprise, of knowing something was in store for her. So, she cleaned up quickly, jumped out of the shower, wrapped her towel around her, and got out of the bathroom running. She stopped in the middle of the living room and looked at David, who was pouring himself a glass of wine.

"What is it? Where is it? Whaaattt?" she screamed with the enthusiasm of a 5-year-old opening a gift on Christmas day.

"Bedroom," said David, laughing.

She ran into the bedroom and saw a big bag from Dior.

"Dior! What is it – why, David!" She took out the extra paper in the bag quickly to see what was inside.

"We already signed, so this is more of a celebratory dinner!"

Vee stopped and looked at him surprised.

"Oh my god, honey, congratulations! This is amazing!"

She threw herself around his neck and kissed him, then a few seconds later, she jumped back to the Dior bag. Finally, she found it: a gorgeous red dress made of silk. She smiled and put it around her body as she turned around to David excited.

"Do you like it?"

"I love it!" Vee said and turned around toward the mirror.

"Great! I bought it for tonight; we're going to RL."

Vee's eyes went immediately toward her calves – the dress was short, just over her knees. She was now faced with an awkward situation: She loved the dress, but if she wore it for dinner, everyone would notice her scars. More importantly, David would.

"OK, hurry up. Now we're really going to be late!" David said, looking at his watch.

But Vee already was in her *big scar cover-up* state of mind. She ran toward the bathroom and opened her drawer under the sink where she held all the stuff she didn't use on a day-to-day basis – tampons, dry shampoo, leg airbrush. She pulled out the leg airbrush and lifted her leg on top of the bathtub edge. Hours of YouTube tutorials of other women hiding their small scars should pay off, she thought. However, unlike those people online, she never really practiced it, or went above and beyond to understand and master the art of concealing a scar. Granted, she had tried it before. She did everything right – the green concealer for the brown side of a scar, the tattoo concealer for the base, airbrush and setting powder to finish it up. On paper, everything worked, but on her calves, it didn't. Her scar was too big for such makeup; it was on the surface of her entire calf.

She always was amused by how much other women would try and conceal a small cut or bruise and always wondered how tough it must be for those with a big scar on their face or who were dealing with acne. Sure, ask anyone or open any magazine, and everybody is all about body positivity and will tell you just how gorgeous you are and how nobody cares. But only you, the one living with the scars, knows just how much everybody actually cares, just how much their eyes are judging you. It's easy to pretend you're woke on Instagram, but it's not that easy to live with it every day.

"Are you ready?" David knocked on the door.

"Just a minute!" Vee screamed at the top of her lungs, in a panic.

"Did you lock yourself in?"

"Just give me a minute, and I'll be out," Vee replied, avoiding his question.

Vee airbrushed her scar, then airbrushed the other calf as well to even things out.

Her calves now looked ridiculous with makeup. They looked yellow and pale as if they were made out of plastic. She took a napkin and tapped it on her legs, trying to take away some of the shining, then finished it up with setting powder and took another look. They still looked plastic.

Vee already was sweating – half from stress, half from needing to hurry up. Her legs looked terrible, and she didn't even put makeup on her face yet.

"Let's go!" David bellowed, again knocking on the door, this time a little annoyed.

Vee rushed to put makeup on, and she looked nothing like she wanted to for this celebratory dinner – her hair was a little curly at the back of her neck from the sweat, her eyebrows weren't brushed equally, and although she was wearing Dior, she looked nothing like she imagined she'd look like in a Dior dress. She had just wasted 15 minutes for nothing and now also needed to clean off the concealer sprayed on her legs and all over the tub. This was just ridiculous, she thought.

Vee had a weird relationship with her scars. When she was alone, she wouldn't really look at them too much, as if she were hiding them from herself too. It's like she also wanted to lie to herself that they weren't there, but given the option to not have the scars, would she have taken it?

For many years, Vee toyed with the idea of having plastic surgery to cover her scars, but the thing with surgery is that it doesn't solve the problem. It can do only two things – either hide the scars or create new ones. She had a friend once with scars a while ago, similar to what she had on her calf. This friend had surgery after surgery to hide them and instead of the scars becoming better, they just morphed into something else.

The idea that a scar would become a different scar was something Vee couldn't conceive. It would be as if she'd be reliving everything again, and that was out of the question. So, she never had surgery. She remembered when she was young, she sent a picture of her scars to a doctor, who told her they seemed infected, but it wasn't a case of infected scars, but rather a bad doctor. However, ever since, she refused to look for an answer.

As time passed, she learned to accept her scars, and they became like a weird self-Stockholm syndrome, in which even though she hated them and felt embarrassed, she wouldn't want to give them up. She had developed a relationship with them. They had become part of her self-identity. Furthermore, she often thought that the scars made her who she is today. Without them, she would've relied on her beauty to help her out in life. She would've done ballet, worn short skirts, maybe even pursued modelling, and she wouldn't have had to struggle to build a career. Maybe she would've married an old man for money and not work a day in her life. On the flip side, she always would've chased that, but her perception of her own beauty would've been perfectly wrong. She would've grown into a frustrated single woman who would die alone with 10 cats, but the scars made her fight for her career and focus on her smarts – not her looks, posture, and appearance – but rather who she was beyond her appearance. You can't just give up a part of yourself because it's not like everything else, especially if that's what has made you.

But that night, in that bathroom, wearing a dress she wouldn't buy for herself, but had to wear, she wanted those scars gone. She took another breath and exited the bathroom – she'd pull it off, like she always did.

George Stanley was one of New York private equity's most well-known figures, a former mergers-and-acquisitions firm owner who became a private equity mogul in just over 10 years. Partnering with George was a huge move for David, even though it was a small venture into the blockchain world. Vee knew that all David wanted was a foot in the door for a further partnership with Pattrick & Stanley, George's main private equity fund.

Being a big shot in Manhattan meant getting the best table pretty much anywhere you wanted, with the most beautiful woman of the year on your arm in Manhattan's richest ZIP code of that year. And George didn't disappoint. Jinx was one of the top restaurants in New York City, and it turned its discreet ambiance into a more stylish version of a champagne party in Courchevel after 10 p.m.

"What happens in Jinx stays in Jinx. Otherwise, you jinx it" was the concierge's welcoming line, hinting at the deals being made in the restaurant and celebrated afterward wildly. Their table was, of course, one of the best tables, overseeing the whole of Manhattan from the 95th floor, with the entire circular bar in the middle that became a stage for acrobats and dancers at night.

"David, my man." George greeted David and Vee with the strongest handshake Vee had felt in years.

"Exciting times, George," David replied, excited.

"Hey, don't jinx it!" George pointed out in a cheesy way, and they both burst into fake laughter. "Meet Courtney, my girlfriend."

Courtney was a gorgeous model and one of New York's socialites of the year. She had dark curly hair, beautiful dark eyes, and legs that went on forever. "Forever" was a pair of crystal-encrusted sandals that lit up the room. She was wearing a gray satin dress with a diamond necklace to match her diamond Patek.

"She's a wellness entrepreneur," George continued.

"Of course she is," Vee thought to herself.

"She's an advertising executive," George told Courtney about Vee. "She's going to be featured in Five for the Next Five by *FW* magazine."

"Oh my god, that's amazing! Congratulations," Courtney replied, then smiled widely at Vee.

Vee smiled back, introduced herself, and sat down at the table. There's nothing more dangerous than silent female competition. Vee and Courtney came from such different worlds and chased such different goals that competition made no sense, but for Vee, it was instinctual. Her defense was always her intellect, but it didn't work for all offense moves out there. And Courtney was one of the best quarterbacks of New York's night life. She was so confident of herself that it seemed like she didn't care much about competition, didn't acknowledge Vee's offense, and was being awfully nice to her. She complimented her dress and entertained Vee through several discussions about traveling, interior designers, and Nasdaq's latest dip. That disarmed Vee. Courtney was a different player, and Vee had to keep up. The reality was that Vee felt very insecure. If women like Courtney were out there – so beautiful, smart, and perfect – how could she keep a man like David near her? How could she acknowledge Courtney for who she was, rather than diminish her value in the eyes of her husband? After a few drinks, she finally found a weak spot in Courtney – she wasn't into extreme sports. On the other hand, George was an avid climber, so Vee took advantage and talked about rock-climbing and the latest peaks that she and David had reached. She lingered on the conversation just enough to bore Courtney and gain a competitive advantage. Vee got so into the conversation that she barely noticed Courtney getting up to leave for the restroom. However, she did notice when she returned.

Vee was sitting right at the edge of the table, her dress lifting all the way above her knees, with her calf scar visible. It was a criminal mistake, a slip that could cost her everything. Courtney was sitting right next to the table, looking at her scar, and was about to speak. For a split second, Vee's heart stopped, blood rushed through her entire body, and she felt like she was about to collapse. Courtney was analyzing her scar, confused.

"What's up honey?" George asked.

"Love your shoes," Courtney said and smiled at Vee.

George pulled up the tablecloth from beneath the table to take a glimpse at her shoes. They weren't as exciting as the ones Courtney was wearing, but he smiled and approved.

"Really nice shoes."

Vee was surprised. There's no way she didn't see the scar; it was staring her in the face. As it turned out, Courtney was the biggest surprise of the evening, and Vee might have just become one of her fans.

"That's very kind, thank you." Vee then smiled back at Courtney.

After two glasses of champagne and some mezcal, Vee started to feel more sexy, confident, and – truthfully – just more drunk. Luckily for her, it was time for George to head home, as he had a call with an investor in China early in the morning, so they had to call it a night.

During the car ride home, Vee was wondering whether Courtney told George or anyone else anything about the scar, and if she didn't, isn't it ridiculous that a stranger knows more about her body than her husband, that a stranger accepts her more than her husband? Her insecurities slowly turned into unprompted anger and unfair disappointment.

David never acknowledged her beauty that night. To be fair, he was more introverted when it came to relationships and extroverted about everything else. "You could tell me I look good," she'd joke every once in a while, as she'd see him looking at how she dressed to go out, to which he protested, "You know you look good; you always look good." But that wasn't enough for Vee – she wanted him to say it proactively and acknowledge what she couldn't acknowledge about herself. But things with David just didn't work that way, as he wasn't the kind of guy you could train in a relationship. Maybe if she told him where all this was coming from, he'd pay more attention, but the stakes were too big, and Vee never really dug down to see which part of her soul this was coming from. Most likely, it wasn't coming from her soul, but her scars.

"Am I beautiful?" Vee just burst out, releasing the energy she could no longer hold inside.

"Stop it," David replied, annoyed, as this wasn't a first-time occurrence.

"No, seriously. Am I beautiful?"

41

"You know you are."

"No, I don't know," Vee interrupted and looked outside her window.

David nodded his head, annoyed.

"Sometimes it feels like you don't know me," she continued.

"How can you say I don't know you? That's ridiculous," David replied, angrily.

"Do you?"

"Yes, I do. We're married. What's up with you tonight?"

"Well, there are things you don't know about me," she mumbled.

"It's not the first time you've said that, and it's starting to be annoying. If you have something to say, just say it. Why are you talking in riddles?"

Vee sat quietly and looked at the lights of Manhattan, flashing intermittently in the distance between the cables of the Brooklyn Bridge.

"There are just things you don't know about me that you'll never know. It's better that way."

"Which things?"

"Nothing. Let it go."

"No, I won't let it go. What do you mean?"

"Well, you don't know stuff – stuff about me."

David turned toward her, now clearly annoyed and somewhat scared.

"Like what? What don't I know?"

Vee was swallowing her words. She felt like she could no longer keep the secret from him. By now, Courtney would have told George anyway. For 23 years, a truth was hidden under the rug, but now it was all coming out, and while she'd been screaming the truth with a mute voice since she met David, he never heard her. Not him, not anybody. It was all her. But now – it was all pouring out, and there was no way to stop it.

"It's like you don't see me."

He sighed and turned around to look outside the window again, realizing she'll just continue like this and never actually answer.

"Like, do you even know what scars I have on my body?"

"What do you mean? Of course I know. You're my wife."

"Oh yeah? Then name them."

"Are you serious? Right now?"

"Yes. Name them."

"On your hand; on your back, while I just noticed it a few days ago when I asked you about it – never noticed it before; and the one on your calf. What, is there any other?"

Vee froze. 23 years crumbled down into her Jimmy Choo sandals and up again as her eyes suddenly teared up. A stone was being lifted off her chest, but nobody was there to witness it. An atomic bomb had been defused quietly and nobody was there to congratulate her on surviving it. The same way it was placed there,

43

the same way it was lifted up. David knew. He knew about all her scars!

For how long? When did he find out? Why didn't he say anything? What did he think about it? All these questions were rushing through Vee's body, but nobody was there to answer.

"So? What do you mean? Tell me, what's the stuff I don't know about you? Tell me, Vee." David continued unaware of the atomic bomb going off inside Vee.

"Nothing…," she blushed.

"I really don't understand you," he continued. David was annoyed again, not understanding why she suddenly went quiet…But for Vee, that was one of the loudest, most important moments of her life.

Chapter 2

Stone

"You can't break the category without breaking your own rules, Mr. Jackson," Stone proclaimed, clenching her fists and looking into his eyes – what already was known as the Stone stare.

"OK...!" Anderson interrupted, clearly irritated by Stone's condescending argument with one of the most prominent CEOs in the Americas. "So, Mr. Jackson, we heard your feedback. Great builds. Let's go back to the agency game plan and circle back with you and the team with the next steps. Sound good?"

Stone couldn't listen to Anderson's bullshit bingo anymore; she just heard a loud ringing in her ears from the mountain of stress that weighed on her shoulders ever since they won this client, and she wouldn't let it go if she wanted to do great work. She felt like this was a client who hired them because he wanted to be challenged and that all the political-niceness suits that Anderson was playing weren't going to fly with Mr. Jackson. Maybe she didn't play her part well, or maybe she had no idea what she was doing. She was angry on the outside, but inside, this anger was molding together with a feeling of happiness and pride, as if she had done what was right. Of course, Anderson came in and took a dump on her reverse-psychology tactic.

"Listen, Mrs. Stone," Mr. Jackson interrupted Anderson, barely hearing his pleading either. "My family is a family of aviators, military personnel. My grandfather started this company after he fought in World War II and had a regiment of 30 under his command. He believed in strong orders to follow, and this is how he built this company; this is why we are who we are today – one of the top 10 aviation companies in the world. It's because of his strong beliefs. My father was wealthy before he was born, just like me, yet he still served in Vietnam because he felt the burden of this legacy and wanted to experience the discipline that gave birth to this company's foundations. I haven't gone to war; I was lucky enough not to have to during my lifetime. But I still believe that it's the rules that keep you disciplined, and it's the discipline that helps you achieve success ...."

"Mr. Jackson, I believe what Mrs. Stone was saying ..."

Anderson interrupted, but Mr. Jackson quickly turned around to him, annoyed":

"If you don't mind, Mr. Anderson, I haven't finished," Mr. Jackson retorted, then continued his argument with Stone, completely dismissing Anderson:

"Now. I like to look at myself as a rebel, an innovator, someone who's ready to do things differently. But Mrs. Stone, I have a duty to follow, you know. I'm not a deserter."

Stone looked straight into his eyes, like a cat waiting for her next move, not knowing where this argument was going. Mr. Jackson stopped his argument and looked at her during the most awkward silence she had felt that year. Cold sweat was dripping from her armpit, sliding into her bra, between her breasts, and she could feel the white silk shirt sticking to her skin. She had no idea where this was going, i.e., whether she had won the argument or just lost her job. In any event, she was already in the fight, so she could only keep on fighting. She decided to hold on to a reply for another breath. She knew that if Mr. Jackson spoke, that would be the end of it – she either would've won or lost, and that would've been the best outcome anyway.

Mr. Jackson, the whitest 60-year-old man in all Kentucky, suddenly smiled as if acknowledging Stone's strength of character and silence.

"However, Mrs. Stone, I can see your passion for this idea, so if you want to work with me on bending some rules, if you think bending them, not breaking them, is good enough for you, I'm ready to go on that journey."

Stone smiled back, knowing she had won the argument:

"So, let's fly, Mr. Jackson."

"That will be all for today," concluded Mr. Jackson, who then got up. Stone, Anderson, and the three other male execs on their team stood up to greet him. Mr. Jackson shook Anderson and his three male execs' hands, concluding with the most senior person in the room – a woman – Stone. A weird room dynamic, but Stone got used to this male-dominated industry in her more-than-15 years of work in advertising, so she wouldn't let pride show anymore. She always knew that if she wanted to succeed, she not only had to learn how to play the game, but also pretend to enjoy it.

As they left the meeting, Anderson's fake attitude congratulating Stone for the presentation made her lose her mind because of his annoying grin. However, years of corporate practice made her smile back at him and excuse herself elegantly to use the restroom. She walked into the bathroom and bent over to see whether she could see the feet of anybody using any of the stalls. Realizing she was alone, Stone walked to the mirror and glanced at herself in the tight suit and silky shirt, which now had become one with her skin. Suddenly, all that high pressure from inside her body became uncontrollable, and she burst into tears – big advertising tears of relief, she thought.

When you've come this far, taking a step back isn't easy. When you're a woman and you've come this far, taking a step back isn't an option. You carry the burden of millions of women looking up to you, as well as the pressure of your own conscience telling you to stay put, stand tall, and that others would kill for your position. But in this mountain of strength that you become, all you need is a little draft to make you crumble into pieces.

Don't be emotional, or you'll seem dramatic. Don't get angry, or you'll be viewed as hysterical. Don't be too tough, or you'll be called a bitch. Don't be too human, or you'll be called weak. Don't have a baby, or you'll flatline. If you're a woman in an EVP position, you're already too far ahead; time for you to slow down. But Stone wasn't ready to slow down.

Stone was referred to as "Stone" for a reason – she was cold, blunt, and tough on people. She was the woman with the pants and could take men on in fistfights if she wanted. Imaginary fistfights, as she was as fragile as a race dog – tall, skinny, long beautiful dark hair – but could chase you to the finish line, though she would be pretty much exhausted at the end. Many men would gossip behind her back that it's beauty gone to waste for the sake of a career, that she was not wife material, and that they pitied her sorry ass of a husband. As if pursuing and fighting for her future were working against her possibility of actually having a family.

Stone wasn't really made out of stones. She heard things, saw things, and wasn't that tough, and all these words were piling up inside her. Behind that tough shell she was carrying around for display, she was a fragile, insecure woman. Nobody knew that, of course, but that executive vice president standing at the big boys table was an Olympic brawler.

But let's back up a little.

Stone had been with her ad agency for a while now – five-and-a-half years – but at the speed the employees' revolving door is moving these days in her industry, she already is viewed as an agency veteran. That would explain why she felt so worn out at times. She didn't know how she ended up in that big position in the first place, what gave her the right to succeed, why they recruited her, and why she rose up the ladder so fast. She questioned whether she was even qualified to be there in the first place. She didn't want to be a PR statistic so that her company could brag in newspapers about being a 50/50 organization. Secretly, while she agreed that there weren't enough women in leadership positions, she didn't want to be thought of as a consequence of the women's movement in the past couple of years. She wanted to know that she really deserved the position she was in, that she wasn't hired to balance out the ratio of a room full of white, middle-aged male executives, but how could she? It would be great for her to know. That would really give her the confidence boost she needed all her life. However, time had taught her that nobody tells you you're good at that level; they're just twisting harsh words to test you out and see whether you're really fit to be in a leadership position.

A series of events helped her achieve her career success. The most crucial aspect was gaining senior leaders' trust. She was articulate, knew when to listen and when to speak, had a high emotional IQ, could read the room faster than most of the world, and was a hard worker. But she always thought that she didn't have that genius, that spark you need to excel in the industry, so she always was confused and unsure when people trusted her, followed her, or when she won. She was the one who apparently doubted herself the most. So, when she achieved success, it always would be because of someone having made a mistake or just pure luck. She just thought it never was based on her merit.

To the outside world, she was good at playing the game. Fighting for industry awards, pushing her teams to get more, and transforming businesses. She was talked about in mass media and was a role model for many women who wanted to make it in the industry, yet she never really felt she was all that, as if her entire professional career had been an out-of-body experience.

Lately, during interviews, it was at a point where she'd doubt what she told others about how great her agency was or about how great the ad industry still is. Deep down, she was facing a serious identity crisis. She sometimes thought perhaps these were all signs of burnout, so she conditioned herself every morning to love her job again because that's all she knew how to do, and that's what made her who she is today. But burnout, demotivation, and mean people eventually get to you, and there's no amount of meditation, self-care, and faith that can keep you on track for too long.

It was in this state of mind that Stone got an email on that May 1 that read: "Fwd: *RFP Amon SLF Pitch.*"

Amon was one of the biggest car manufacturers in the world, and they had entered the market with a fully electric car. In the early years, everyone was mocking their model and their vision. Most thought the market wasn't ready for it yet and that no amount of design could compensate for lack of availability from the market. However, California always has been a different kind of state, and people always have embraced what's possible. So, as the years passed by and adoption grew, Amon became a category leader. They were now ready for the next big step – autonomous cars – another big bet on their end in an otherwise very skeptical market, perhaps even more than before. Ethics and safety questions arose immediately after they announced their prototype, and social media was buzzing with all the risk this model could bring on the streets. So, a pitch of this kind would be not just a first for the agency, but quite frankly a first for the entire industry.

The email – well, to be fair, the forwarding of an email – came from her boss, Daniel, which explains why it was forwarded in the first place. Usually, he didn't bother to write too much about what something like this was or at least give her a heads-up. Stone had to read through the entire email history – through cc's, replies, and half-baked thoughts about random people – to understand what this request was all about. His short blurb in the forward read *"You're leading this, Stone."* That was it.

This was definitely a great opportunity for Stone, and she was going to grab it – the big break she was waiting for. A big piece of business for a big client against big agencies, and she was up to the challenge. Even if it meant less sleep or personal life and not doing anything else for the next couple months, she wanted this client. It was her chance to beat CDV and Velocity5, the leading creative agencies in the world. She was about to sit at the table with the big boys and show them what she's got. The next day, she was on a plane to San Diego.

Stone loved to fly. Contrary to most execs who fly so much that they eventually end up loathing it, she actually enjoyed every minute of it. She loved everything about the little ritual before leaving her house – packing her aluminum Rimowa with work essentials, filling her little Mont Blanc pen with ink, placing a bookmark in her leather notebook. She was organized that way and liked to keep things neat. Her glorious suits were waiting for her in her big dressing room, and she was quite superstitious about which one to wear. Dark green was some sort of good luck charm for her, so every time she needed self-confidence and a bit of luck, she always went for dark green. She learned from a visit in Shanghai a few years ago that many people view red, yellow, and green as lucky colors, but that yellow and red would put her at a significant disadvantage in a room filled with men, so as with many things in life as a woman, she compromised with green. Luckily, green started to grow on her. There's something about wearing nice clothes for an important meeting that made her feel more confident. It was kind of cliche, but Stone always believed cliches were underrated. She had to be original in her day job, so she found comfort in the most mainstream things. The clothes she was wearing, the lipstick she was putting on, the fake glasses – everything was stagecraft. Not for clients, but for her psyche. When she looked the part, she acted the part, and everybody respected her.

Her palms were already sweaty as the flight prepared to land, and she gazed outside the window looking over San Diego. She wondered who else on the plane was there for the same Amon meeting. She didn't know all the stakeholders in Velocity5 or CDV, but the agencies were all based in New York, so at least a few definitely would be on the same flight. There's a certain kind of arrogance in business class that's proprietary to airplanes. A wide cast of rich corporate execs, point collectors, and surprise upgrades all rub shoulders as if they were made from the same cloth. The rich don't notice those around them; it's nothing special to them. The corporate always will give you the look, as if to convey they made it, and you haven't. The point collectors are the most uptight, dressed nicely and desperately trying to fit in, and may even strike up a conversation. The surprise upgrade is always a surprise, but Stone knew you can identify them as those who mimic moves and order the most. At 30,000 feet, imposture and arrogance blend together.

The man seated next to her held an *Economist* magazine issue, folded between his right leg and the armrest. A great decoy for a business flier desperately trying to point out he's an intellectual, while enjoying some sort of Candy Crush-type game on his mobile instead of actually reading the magazine. As the man confirmed her business class decoy theory, she smiled, imagining sitting next to this guy at the debriefing session. Then, following yet another cliché in her life, she blasted the music in her headphones as the plane descended in San Diego. Perfect timing for the wheels to hit the ground while the lyrics from Sia's "Unstoppable" were playing.

As she walked into Amon's lobby with Anderson, she paused. She was expecting a high-tech, imposing, look-at-us kind of lobby. Instead, she got quite a dull welcome in return. The building seemed to have been built in the '70s, and it had a rusty look to it.

"Quite the contradiction…" Anderson said as he gazed around, as surprised as Stone. Stone smiled and took her entry badge from the reception desk. As they walked toward the elevators, Stone noticed pictures of the Amon family on the wall. Amon had a modern history in the automobile industry, quite atypical for the San Diego market. Stone noticed Amon Sr. repairing a car somewhere in Morocco, where the Amon family was from. They were known for being one of the richest immigrant families in America, carrying forward a tradition of mechanical engineers inherited from North Africa. As they went up to the 15th floor, Stone couldn't help but wonder if the building wasn't a coincidence: What if it wasn't a slight from a greedy management? What if it was quite the opposite? She started to believe that the reason why this very building has been kept intact was because that's how Peter Amon, CEO and chairman of the organization, wanted to honor the company's automobile engineering history.

"If that's the case, it's quite a corny juxtaposition," Stone thought.

They exited the elevator and entered the conference room, where Stone immediately spotted the Candy Crush guy from the plane. "No fucking way," she thought and smiled to herself, realizing that he was so absorbed in the game that he didn't realize she had been sitting right next to him all that time.

Like in a boxing ring, agency folks don't shake hands before a pitch, introduce each other, or even acknowledge themselves in front of the client. In theory, none of them knew which agency the other was from. In practice, they all did. In reality, they were all too arrogant, including Stone.

Peter Amon was a third-generation immigrant – the best kind of immigrant, he thought, because he didn't have to go through the hurdles his grandfather did to fit into the United States, nor deal with the identity crisis his dad experienced while growing up. As a third-generation immigrant, his goal was to expand and become a true American power to prove that his family was more than an immigration story – a point of growth for their adoptive economy.

Stone was at a disadvantage in this race. She wasn't an immigrant, unlike some of her rivals at the table. She was born on the East Coast, was white, and had all the privilege. At least in theory. Her only real edge at that table was that she was the only woman to be leading the creative process. That might matter, but Peter Amon was a man who didn't seem deterred by this small detail. Granted, he was right.

The brief seemed exciting to her. Peter Amon was charming, intelligent, and knew autonomous cars and machine learning inside and out. He could school anybody on machine ethics and the impossibility of finding a universal moral code for cars. He prided himself on the patent that they had acquired for the SLF model.

Stone wasn't necessarily a car freak. She always picked a car based on looks and comfort, never by engine power or gadgetry. The more they talked, the more she felt like an odd pick for this pitch.

While others were jotting down questions for the client, she already was writing thought starters for the work she could sell and thinking of the right team for this and how to break through the category. Then again, maybe all the others were doing the same thing.

"Who's your target, Mr. Amon?" Velocity5's account director asked.

"Well, it's everybody who can afford it, really. Our research showed men are more inclined to buy self-driving cars, as they're more interested in how a vehicle operates," Amon replied.

"However, we don't want to alienate women," Amon's marketing executive added.

"What a stupid question," Stone thought to herself. "Do your homework, man."

When the meeting ended, and they all bid Amon farewell, Stone danced again to the corporate music and shook the CEO's hand last. After all, she was still the only woman at the table.

***

There's something proprietary about the creativity process. The first 48 hours after receiving a brief are filled with enthusiasm. Creative ideas fly in, and there's nothing that can stop you from finding the best in-class ad you're looking for. Stone always believed in using the time immediately after a briefing to jot down ideas that flew in, trusting her creative gut. She called this creative detox because out of the dozen ideas she generated at this point in the process, at best one would survive until the client presentation. Most of the bad, low-hanging fruit would disappear.

That morning, Stone woke up energized. It was a beautiful day in New York, she kissed her husband goodbye, and headed to her nice office in the Financial District. On one hand, she always found it odd that the ad agency was in a financial district, instead of the Williamsburg area or at least SoHo. On the other hand, it kind of made sense. Advertising was no longer sex, drugs, and rock 'n' roll. It was more like accountants, data, and audiences. What the hell happened to the power of a good old creative idea? Advertising was now as corporate as it got, and it came with all the corporate benefits – long meetings, no work-life balance, and no pay raises.

Endless meetings with the strategy team, the politics of Anderson's account management, and all the bullshit behind making ads would come into play more often, and her ideas would never see the light of day. Instead, they would die a slow, painful death that all agency ideas do.

What many people fail to tell you when you take the fast track up the corporate ladder is that while you do skip over many career years, those years come back to you in concentrated, atomic-like bursts of stress that manifest through your insecurities. So, it's harder to fight and harder to argue, particularly if you have an always-on kind of attitude that will only lead to burnout. How do you melt down and talk about burnout? You don't. You're an executive and can't be burned out. People look up to you, so you gotta send the elevator back down for them. But how do you send it down when you barely can reach the buttons?

"I need to get Taylor and Jason on the Amon SLF pitch," Stone told her resource manager as she entered the office.

Taylor and Jason were one of the agency's creative director superstar teams. Stone brought them to the agency and mentored them into becoming one of the most coveted teams in the industry. However, it became increasingly difficult for her to get them scoped on any projects, as they were always busy working with the other ECDs, Steve White and Bobby Lipcinski. Stone was getting along great with Steve and Bobby, but while to some it was pure coincidence and to others, it was because they played golf with Daniel, their requests always superseded hers.

"Shoot. I'm sorry, Stone, but their workload is already ridiculous. They're in production with Steve and Bobby, kicking off two projects with them on the food business," said the resource manager. "What about Jessie and Terrell?" she suggested.

"They're great, but not senior enough. I need at least two directors to help win this. Come on, Shannon, this business is important to the agency. Why do I always have to beg for resources?" Stone objected.

"What can I tell you? Maybe it would be a good idea to chat with Daniel. Maybe he can help prioritize with Steve and Bobby."

Stone hated office politics. Daniel Cohen was the CCO – a nice guy, but arguably not the most talented fellow in the industry. He liked to surround himself with people who wouldn't question his superiority, and more so his talent. Daniel inherited Stone, i.e he came in with Stone already well-regarded in the agency and industry, so it would be impossible for him to push her out. At least it wouldn't be a good idea. She had the team's vote of confidence, and she knew how to dance the corporate tango, so Daniel pretended to be nice, while Stone let him think he can lead the way. Neither were fans of dancing, but the music already was loud, others were already on the floor, and this was out of their control. Thus, they pretended they knew how to tango. Stone dreaded the idea of going to Daniel, but knew this was her only way in.

Daniel had long hair and a smile that could light up a room. He was brought up by a Brazilian dad and Lebanese mom. He was a charming second-generation immigrant and knew how to tick off the boxes of a senior executive. Although he lacked creative talent, he had just enough charisma to charm a client's room and sell pretty much anything, which, it turns out, sometimes was more important than being able to assess a good idea. Stone respected that, but she also was craving a mentor, though some might say that at age 35, you should be your own mentor, i.e., do less learning and more teaching.

"Hey, Daniel, got a minute?" Stone barged into his office after knocking two times on his door, not even giving him time to invite her in.

"For you always, Stone, what's up?" Daniel replied, a bit taken aback.

"I need your help to get senior talent scoped on the Amon SLF pitch," Stone said firmly.

"Whom do you need?"

"Taylor and Jason."

"Hmm. I believe they're working with Bobby on the food business."

"I know, Daniel, but they're always working with Bobby on the food business. I can't win this pitch without strong talent."

"OK, let me talk to Ashley," Daniel reassured her.

Ashley was his right hand, doing the jobs he didn't want to do — actually handling the human resources in the department. She was a very lovely woman, Stone thought, but she was being pushed around by all the other creative directors. Stone knew there's nothing more she could do because whenever she needed to negotiate new teams with Bobby, she'd lose.

Stone was trapped in a corporate loop in which she couldn't handle resources on her own; her boss didn't have the resources to help her, yet he wanted her to win the pitch; and she just didn't have an ally. But just like a goldfish, Stone always went into a new project with enthusiasm, thinking she'll get the help she needs. To be honest, that was the only way she could survive and grow, by being more like Dory in Finding Nemo and continuously swimming with a positive attitude.

"Hey, Stone. What's up?" Taylor popped into her office. "I hear you want us on a pitch? Cool stuff?"

"Hey, Taylor. Yes, keeping my fingers crossed you guys can jump on it," Stone replied, excited to see Taylor. After all, it's been a while since they last worked together.

"Listen, I told Ashley I want to work on it. I'm sick of working just on the food business. Jason is pretty fed up with it too." Taylor said, closing the door behind her, making it obvious this information and whatever comes afterward shouldn't leave Stone's office. "This fucking guy, Stone, I can't stand him anymore. He has no vision, has no real feedback, and couldn't spot a good idea if it hit him in the head."

Stone listened without reacting, just smiling and nodding. After all, she was an executive of that agency and couldn't say anything, even though she completely agreed with Taylor. However, she never really wanted to play the women vs. men card, even though she felt it, and it hurt her too. However, she always wanted work, not politics, to lead the way.

It's really lonely at the top, particularly if you're a woman. There are not enough women to go out for cocktails with after work in this field, no C suite golf club for women, no blowing off some steam with other CEOs. You don't rub shoulders and bitch about your employees, not if you're a woman – not because you don't want to or because for some God-given reason you don't feel the need to, but simply because there's no one you can do that with. When you're a woman, it's really, really, really lonely and depressing at the top.

Stone wasn't the motherly type either. For some reason, they say women lead differently, that they have more of a nurturing style. Stone disagreed with that, but maybe it was just her own personal bias. She was an introvert and really lived by her name. And let's be honest, you can't really cluster women's management styles into one box. After all, men do lead differently among themselves too, using different management styles.

"I'm telling you, Stone, if I don't work on a different project soon, I'm gonna call it quits. I've had enough." Stone felt responsible for Taylor even after so many years and didn't want her to leave the agency. The reality of the work force isn't what you see in movies, in which people come and go, and the executives don't care at all. Stone knew that every time someone left, it was like a stab to the heart of the company's well-being.

Stone was a manager, a creative type, a wife, and a therapist now to everyone who walked into her office to vent – but who cared about her emotions? Who cared about what Stone wanted? This wasn't some start-up she had built; she wasn't a shareholder earning a big bonus. And yet, nobody had ears for her. There was very little conversation about how prone C suite was to depression. Being successful is a blessing and a curse. Once you've arrived to where you wanted to be, it's harder to overcome your status, and it's lonelier than on your way up. Moreover, you can suffer from the "oh, poor little rich kid" syndrome: Just as kids from rich families aren't allowed to complain because they were born into families of privilege, people who've made it can't complain because they're far better than many of the rest.

"I understand, Taylor," said Stone, barely managing her own emotions. "This project is really exciting; there's a chance we will revolutionize how people think about self-autonomous cars. We're standing on the edge of the opportunity to change how we position a car brand and who we talk to." She continued very seriously. She always used corporate jargon to balance anger and frustration.

"Well, that's dope. We'll crush it," Taylor whispered naively, almost as if she didn't want anyone else to hear about the project and work on it. She slowly closed the door behind her and left Stone with a big forced smile on her face, pretending she's excited as well.

OK, truthfully, she was excited about the opportunity and competition. She also was terrified. After so many years of corporate wars, Stone also hated the game a bit. She hated having to go through so many loops within the organization to make something happen. It was the process that was draining her the most, not actually doing the work. Sometimes, she forgot that this process was part of the job too, and she mastered it.

"Wanna get pizza tonight?" Stone texted her husband, trying to escape the reality of the grind.

"Shitty day already?" he replied.

Stone looked at the phone and scrolled up to read previous conversations with her husband. Between countless lifeless emojis sent in a hurry between meetings were traces of logistics of a marriage and very little about the romance of a relationship. There, laid as testimony of a life devoted to career, was a string of messages like "Sorry, I'll be late tonight." "Can't answer. Meeting. Can you text?" "Is it urgent?" "Can we order in?" Stone didn't need a therapist to tell her a marriage is something you continuously work on; she already knew that. But her career was also part of who she was – part of her identity. To an outsider, that could look a little sad, but it's what she worked on for years and years, and it has molded her into what she has become today – a young, successful female executive. After all, Stone thought, anybody can get married, but not anybody can get a corner office on the 38th floor on Madison Avenue.

"No. I just feel like pizza tonight. Pizza and a good glass of Rioja," Stone answered, trying to change the tone of the chat with her husband.

"Sounds like a date to me," her husband texted back.

"You'd better wait for me with flowers then. ;)," she texted back, smiling at the screen.

"Don't push it, Stone," he replied. She laughed and closed her laptop. Her husband never called her Stone, but when he did, it was intentional, and it was always to make fun of her power play games or work whining.

Finding men to have sex with when you're a female executive isn't that hard. Stone knew how to play the game and how to sell herself. After all, she was in advertising. However, finding a man who will be in a relationship with a female executive? That's a different story. Most single women in New York – and quite frankly, the world – are career women. "They're married to their job," most men say. "Well fuck you, Billy," Stone thought many times. Billy was a random name she had picked to represent all misogynistic men. "Is it OK for a man to stay late at work and juggle kids and corporate, but it's not OK for a woman?" The problem with having a career as a woman these days is not even that you don't have time for your man; it's that you rarely reach that stage. Men have developed this amazing ability to flee before even finding out that you'd make time for them. Careers had become the antidote to a healthy relationship, or perhaps they always were.

When Stone was a junior, she loved to talk about her advertising career. She was a copywriter who wrote hip lines and could point up at billboards in Times Square and say "I made that." Back then, it was cool. Just the right amount of work a woman should be doing, right? The kind of work that could get you a pat on the shoulders or that your boyfriend could brag about over a beer with friends. But not the kind of work that would make men feel threatened. Not the kind of work that would threaten their financial superiority or their ego as a man. That's a different kind of work, and it comes with a senior title – and that's when things get complicated. Over the years, Stone moved from bragging about being this cool, hip junior copywriter in New York to just vaguely answering, *"I'm in advertising."* Many times, she avoided giving out her last name for the first couple of dates so that men couldn't Google her. Web searches and social media ushered in an era of no privacy, so her name was out of the box pretty fast, and men would be out of sight as soon as they saw *"female executive."*

When she met her husband, he was different. Just like a true Leo – the sign, not the actor – he really believed in himself. He had the confidence she could never gain in a lifetime. He was bossy, firm, and it was everything she needed – someone to run her life, as she was sick and tired of running others' lives. When you find someone who will accept you for who you are, you make an effort too. You accept all the flaws in return. Perhaps that's why Stone believed that in many cases, these women are cheated on most often, yet they still stick with the relationship. Perhaps she had become one of them.

When she got home that night, the pizza was cold, the bottle of Rioja was opened, and her husband had fallen asleep on the couch watching Netflix. Stone looked at him, sighed, kissed him on the forehead, and awakened him, like she always did, to send him to the bedroom. The next day, things will go back to square one. She sat down at the table and opened her laptop, like a bad tic she had developed over the years. Right there, at the top of her inbox, was an email from *FW* magazine – one of the leading business and lifestyle magazines in the world. Some of the biggest celebrities, businesspeople, entrepreneurs, and politicians have been on the cover of that magazine, and though lately, social media algorithms made it seem like everybody deserves a medal for any tiny accomplishment, this one was a bit different.

"You've been selected as one of the five women to be featured on our cover edition of Five for the Next Five." She read it out loud, a sign of complete exhaustion, as if actually hearing the words would help her register the message's content faster.

The Five for the Next Five was one of the most coveted honors for women in the business world. Every year, they pick an industry and feature the best female talent that's out there – the movers and shakers, the big shots. Stone was one of them now. She smiled proudly and looked at her husband, hoping he'd wake up so she could share the news. However, the loud snoring proved to be the only reaction she'd get from him tonight.

**

Two weeks into the pitch process, Stone started to feel the pressure. Anxiety was building, and the uncertainty of whether the teams would come up with a winning creative solution was eating her confidence alive. As soon as she opened her email, ad news briefings would pop up, and one day, there was news about Velocity5 – they had won the most awards in the past decade as an independent agency.

"Fuck," Stone thought to herself.

On one level, it was no surprise. She knew they were in a different league and were amazing, but right now, in the middle of her pitch? That's not going to be good. They'll sell that card inside and out, and Peter Amon seemed like just the guy who would buy it. She texted her admin: "Please have the creative teams working on the Amon SLF meet me in my office in 15 minutes. Tell them to bring their new ideas."

Stone assembled two creative director teams: Taylor and Jason, and Fernando and Zayan. Taylor and Jason used to be her right hand, but Fernando and Zayan had been trained by Bobby, so they were more resistant to Stone's way of managing the process. Nevertheless, they were very talented, and Fernando produced the best art direction at the entire agency. They already had a winning idea that Taylor and Jason brought in the first week after briefing day, but wanted to have at least one more to show to Peter Amon.

One way to approach the process was through a path less taken – a risky one Stone really believed in. Instead of focusing on SLF as an autonomous, robotic process, Stone decided to focus on SLF as individuality, as your way to live your life, and more importantly, focus on women. All cars manufacturers talk to men, Stone thought. Even when they talk to women, they talk through a man's mouth.

"Think about it," Stone told Daniel Cohen as she was selling him on the approach. "Every time you see a sports car ad, who's driving it? A man. A suburban van? A mom, a soccer mom, seen through the eyes of a man. A regular car, maybe a Toyota? Yeah, could be a woman because that's what a decent woman could afford, right? Have you seen an ad for a Porsche in which a woman drives the car? Or a big powerful S class?" she continued enthusiastically.

Daniel smiled, knowing where she was going with this and played along, nodding that he had not seen an ad like that.

"I want the SLF to be the first car that speaks to women's self-identity, that can accommodate whatever path a woman takes. We're complex; we multi-taskers; we have careers, families, and friends; and we need control and freedom simultaneously. SLF is exactly that. It can give you the freedom you want when you want it – whether it's because you can drive it how you like to drive, or because it can drive you safely when you have to do 100 things at a time. SLF doesn't come from SLF driving; it comes from your SLF identity," Stone argued. "Amon SLF. Your SLF. Your Driving Style."

Daniel liked Stone's idea, but reminded her that they couldn't go into the pitch with just one creative direction. It was just not customary in the advertising industry pitch process. As the days passed by, no new ideas rose to the top. None found the balance between robotics and humanity, between lifestyle and control. Things weren't looking good.

"We need new teams, Daniel. These ones are burned out." Stone kept pushing on, but as it happens with most projects like this, Daniel promised she'd get more help, yet that never happened.

Without the teams suspecting anything, as they walked into her office, her heart stopped. She was anxious.

"Your right hand, your assistant, not just a passenger, but a co-driver. SLF: Safety, love, fun. We'll hold the wheel for you. It's not the destination – it's the journey." Taylor started to brainstorm instead of presenting something coherent to Stone.

"There's nothing there." Stone argued. "We gotta push, guys. We need new angles."

She could see Bobby in his office sensing her anxiety and smiling at her. He was surrounded by three teams working on a day-to-day project. She smiled back at him, a friendship offering. As he finished the meeting, he walked by her office and popped in:

"Hey, let me know if you need any help on the pitch. Happy to provide my mediocre skill," he said with a smirk on his face that angered Stone.

"Thanks, Bobby. We've got this!" Stone replied, with a coldness that made her win her name. "Oh, and hey, Bobby – fuck you!" she continued in her head.

The professional creative block is one of the most stressful kinds of blocks because you're paid to be creative, and you learn all the thinking patterns and tricks, but there are times when nothing works. You can take all the long showers you want – ideas won't strike. There's no magic "aha" moment in the middle of a commute – no split-second idea when you just need a pen to write something down on a piece of paper. There's none of that. That's in the movies. In real life, it's sometimes just silence. A moratorium on creativity.

"What if we treat this car like any other car? What if instead of making a fuss about the autonomous side of it, we talk about everything else but that?" Zayan asked.

"What do you mean?" Taylor replied.

"Think about it. The moment you put autonomy at the center, it becomes the only criterion you'd buy this car for, and that's the issue – it's so controversial. Yes, that's the differentiator, but what if we bend the rules this time? What if we talk about everything but autonomy?"

"But then what's the selling point?" Jason asked.

"Interesting – go on, Zayan," Stone interjected.

"I mean, think about all new tech products and how they launched – they created scarcity. Think about Gmail. Think about Clubhouse. You had to know someone in the club to get in; someone would have to send you an invite for you to get in."

"I'm not tracking," Taylor jumped in.

"Sorry, I'm jumping from one thing to another. What if, to sell Amon SLF, instead of talking about autonomous driving, we talk about the car and the experience any car should have in the 20th century? The safety, the comfort, the freedom to move at your own pace. And then, to make it more desirable, we open up sales just to a select few who can invite others to buy the car. This will focus attention on why this car is so desirable and less on the controversy of autonomy and ethics of self-driving cars." Zayan continued, confident his rambling will get to a point in the end. "Don't talk about the elephant in the room."

Stone sat quietly listening, staring outside at the Chrysler Building. It was her way of focusing, getting lost in the complexity of its architectural style, on the curves at the top and the windows that looked so small from where she sat. She liked where Zayan was going with the idea.

"I think it's bold, but make sure you land on autonomy. Let's give it a try. Zayan and Fernando, work on this. Let's meet in 48 hours and see how you've evolved it. Taylor, Jason, next time we meet, I want to see scripts and boards on the initial SLF identity direction, something new worth sharing."

As the teams left the meeting, her phone rang.

"Don't forget about Patrick tonight!" her husband texted.

"Shit! Pattrick," She thought and texted back: "Totally. Will try to be back earlier to be able to change for it."

Three dots then started playing on the screen, so her husband was texting back, but taking his time to write the proper answer.

"Remember, it's a cocktail event," he replied, quite a short text considering how long it took him to type it, she thought.

She double-pressed on his text to like his message, to signal that she saw it. After that week, a drink or two would do her well, she thought to herself, then picked up her bag and left the office. It was good for her, she thought. At least she got to spend some more time with her husband, as the past few weeks have been just insane. The party was supposed to be filled with some other ad folks she heard about, big-name executives as well, so like in any advertising party, she had to dress up in her tightest ego and show up as if she ruled the world.

Over the following weeks, as they developed the pitch, nights became more sleepless. She started constantly dreaming she was being chased by someone. It was a dream she used to have when stress piled up. Stress came in the shape of an action movie, as she was either chased by some sort of killer, or by the police for something she didn't do, or else she was desperately trying to catch a flight or pass an exam she didn't study for. Sometimes she dreamed she was unable to stay awake during a meeting or that her eyes fell asleep. Other times, she was naked, or barefoot, and embarrassed. All signs of anxiety and stress, a friend once told her. One could argue they're also a sign of deep, profound insecurity and a feeling of imposture that stuck with Stone all her career.

Unfortunately, anxiety was such a huge part of success. Waking up in the morning with her chest beating – boom-boom, boom-boom – plus sweaty palms and uncontrollable tics that she could not stop were all part of the game. You kind of know why you feel that way, but you still can't control it. All those years of meditation practice gone to waste; all those books she read never found a spot in her subconscious. Sleeping six hours a night and pretending it's fine were part of her identity. Stone always pondered about those articles on famous CEOs who sleep so little and do so much being cited as role models. Well, she had a different theory that wasn't as glamorous as these publications made it sound: "You know why they sleep so little?" She argued with her friends. "Because they're so goddamned stressed out. Look at the palms of their hands. I bet you many of them have psoriasis flare-ups every other month. They can't show it in any other way, but your body can't hide it forever.

When you Google books about female CEOs, you find all these super-woman stories about women who can swing both family and work, who fight, are decisive – and are stone cold. That's what people thought she was as well, but all she wanted to do was to go on Amazon and comment on every single one of those books: "BS! This is what corporate America demands you look like – show no weakness, or you're rendered unfit for the position."

It had been just over a month since they found a second creative direction for the project, but internal meetings were piling up, and the stress wasn't going anywhere. Bobby had taken back all his team's support, but Daniel Cohen was promising Stone more support – though in reality offered nothing. Caught between lack of time and lack of teams, Stone had to get into the work herself. It's funny how all books about leadership tell you not to micromanage, but in her industry, lack of resources went against all rules. Perhaps that's why everyone was complaining about leadership in the industry, she thought.

That morning, all her team's ideas were up on the walls like a beautiful gallery waiting for a buyer – not necessarily for a buyer who could understand art, but who had the means to get it. Daniel Cohen always viewed himself and his job as a form of art, so he imposed this process in which for big presentations, teams would put their work up on the walls, and the executive leaders would review them and put red dots next to each idea they liked and that they felt should move forward to client presentations. He liked this way of providing feedback, no questions asked, as if he was the biggest advertising guru, in which his opinion is never challenged, just embraced. Personality cult? Welcome to advertising.

Stone walked into the agency's hallway and looked at all the ideas hanging on the walls. They looked stunning. The team had stayed up the previous night to have them ready for the 8 a.m. executive meeting. Each campaign was placed on a different wall to ensure they were easy to follow as you pass through the hall, from the moment you see the first message all the way to getting your car keys at the end of the hall. A true user experience, reimagined to Daniel Cohen's delight.

Stone's palms already were sweating. It was something quite uncontrollable. She'd been working with the executive team for a long time, yet every meeting made her really anxious. With five minutes to spare before the meeting was to begin, she rushed to the restroom to freshen up. Her heart suddenly started to beat more rapidly, her breathing was heavier and heavier, faster and faster, and as she looked at herself in the mirror, trying to fight back anxiety, a heat wave suddenly took over her entire body. Starting from her belly all the way up to her chest, then suddenly, out of nowhere, she felt terribly nauseated. Her body was sweating all over at this point. It was already 8 a.m., and she was going to be late, but this was totally uncontrollable. She rushed into one of the stalls and threw up – surprising yet expected simultaneously. Together with half of her guts, she expelled the anxiety over the biggest pitch of her career, comprising the pressure from competing against the two biggest agencies and the hopelessness of having her work being evaluated internally by someone who wasn't able to assess what good work looks like. It was kind of the worst situation she'd been in. Stone held her hand up against the wall, and as she looked at the toilet bowl at 8:01 a.m., she thought: "Damn it, you're behaving like a junior." She washed her hands and face, and cleaned her mascara after the sweat made her look like a crying clown. "Pull your shit together," she thought, took two deep breaths, and exited through the ad gallery.

As she emerged, she looked like nothing happened and was desperately trying to play poker face and show no emotion.

"Ooooo, Stone. Chillax, don't be so tensed. We've got you," said Daniel, relaxed, as if he was a savior.

Stone smiled and said nothing as she watched Daniel and Michael, the CEO, walking around the ideas and placing red dots on the work.

"You all right?" Taylor whispered.

"All good, thanks," Stone replied.

She was feeling a bit ill lately, but every time she felt ill or something personal was happening to her, she had to pick up the phone. At this career level, you can't leave a call unanswered, switch off, and say no. Truthfully, Stone felt bad every time she abandoned her team. She once saw this picture of an iceberg representing anxiety going viral on the Internet. At this point, she was showing all the signs of chronic anxiety – she was on edge, lacked focus, was over-planning, and started to get jumpy. But now throwing up? This was a whole new level.

"Hey, Stone, you with us?" Daniel laughed. "I love what we did with this script on SLF identity."

"Yes, the team did a great job with it," Stone replied, intentionally using "team," not "we."

After all, Daniel was seeing it for the first time and was never curious about how the whole process was going. Stone took another deep breath, realizing she perhaps didn't need to go head to head with her boss at this point in the process.

"Looks great, Daniel!" Michael said. *"You killed it again, Danny. Let's go win this sucker."* He patted Daniel on the back, then Daniel smiled and thanked him with an invisible Namaste sign he learned from a yoga class in SoHo. He embodied all the cultural appropriations that would make Stone vomit, but luckily, she was done with that for the day. As revolting as the theatre aspect of all this was, it actually turned out to be a great review with the leadership team. However, these kinds of meetings made Stone question whether corporate life was right for her and made her question what's next. Figuring out what's next at this level was the most complicated thing. The doors that open are fewer, and they

rarely open. If she wanted to take the next career step, she had to do something on her own.

She wished she had the passion others had to pursue the ideas they believed in. Stone toyed a lot with the idea of opening her own agency, trying her own thing, doing it her own way. However, something always held her back – she never was brave enough to do it. And yet, when she looked around, it seemed like everyone else was doing it. Did you ever want to buy a car you couldn't afford, and now wherever you looked, someone else was driving that car? Well, when you're in the corporate world and want to go solo, it's pretty much the same experience. However, the industry and LinkedIn made everything seem like a joke anyway. Now every job was celebrated; every position was a thing. Either success was the biggest commodity of the 2020s, or it was just a big corporate conspiracy to keep people stuck like hamsters on timesheet wheels. She dreamed about maybe becoming a writer or opening a flower shop. She dreamed dreams she was too tired to pursue, but dreams didn't work unless she was willing to work for them.

She Googled every other day "when is it the right time to start a business" as if she was waiting for divine intervention to tell her to let go. At times, she started to pursue ideas of her own the same way she did with the gym: She bought clothes for the gym thinking that's actually what will make her stick to it, and did the same thing with all entrepreneurial endeavors – find names, do branding for those projects, but quickly lost interest because other executive duties took over. Too many times, she pushed side hustles too much to the side, but maybe this was an advertising trait. She got used to ideas being born, then killed by clients so easily that she didn't like to get too attached and be heartbroken by losing one of her favorites.

Entrepreneurial dreams became northern stars that she entertained once every six months, when things would go sideways and the going got tough. But then work took over, life took over, and she convinced she was OK where she was. After all, others would kill to be in her position.

"Don't you just love it when Danny just takes the credit for everything?" Taylor whispered as she walked by Stone. "Just wait for those awards – see who walks on stage," she continued louder this time as she stepped out of the ad gallery.

Stone smiled and turned around to the empty gallery. In front of her was a script with a red dot that Daniel liked. She read through it and took it apart. She actually hated that script, but it was her fault she left it there.

"How are you feeling?" her husband texted.

"Good … Had a good meeting."

"That's not what I asked."

"I'm good. I hate this fucking guy."

"…" her husband keeps typing. *"Babe…"*

"I keep thinking about that LA offer."

"You know I can't leave New York."

She wants to type back, but soon her husband texts again.

"Any other news?"

She wants to type something elaborate back, but all she can manage to reply is "No."

"OK, please let me know if anything changes."

Stone took another look at her phone, then threw it on her desk, annoyed.

She had an offer in Los Angeles to go run an entire agency for North America, but if you're a woman, you can't make such indecent requests from your husband. The emancipation of women didn't cover situations like this, in which the woman asks the man to relocate and financially support their well-being. This issue just didn't exist at the beginning of the 20th century, when women were happy just because they got voting rights. A century later, society wasn't ready yet to accept that a respectable man would give up his career for a woman. The other way around, yes, of course. It always has been the way of the world. There are no relocation packages that actually help you accommodate the new living scenario for a partner who wants to work, to restart again and again, as if in another corporate conspiracy, in which only one person can be successful in a family, and more often than not, that person is a man.

They toyed around with the idea of moving many times when Stone was feeling down and discussed the topic, but in reality, if

Stone decided to move, it would be a choice between her marriage or her career. To her, there's nothing to choose from – family always came first. Contrary to what everyone believed, she'd never sacrifice love for work. So, the next best thing was the idea of opening her own business, but she didn't have the courage to do it. She just pretended to be tough.

"Maybe it's time to start my own thing," she texted her husband.

"Oh. We talked about this," he replied, as if he had heard this so many times before.

"How could I know if I never try it? I have to grab life and run with it."

"It's not that easy. Others would kill to have the salary you have."

"Well, others don't have to put up with Daniel."

"Trust me, they do. Everybody has his own Daniel. Entrepreneurs, clients, even Steve Jobs had a Daniel at one point. Just so happens his name was John."

Stone knew her husband was right, but it would just piss her off that he wouldn't just openly say, "Hey, you know what? Go for it. I'll support you. We're two in this; we'll do it together." She never actually got that support, or at least she never got the support that she was looking for. As she sat down at her computer, she opened the email from the No Place Like Venice agency in LA. The subject, a testimony of her career, laid there waiting for her to acknowledge it " –President & Chief Creative Officer offer from No Place Like

Venice, LA." She suddenly felt this inner urge to reply and prove her agency, husband, and New York wrong. She would take revenge on people who never hurt her in the first place, or at least didn't realize they did. Or did she just need change?

"That's fucking stupid," she thought, then closed her laptop.

Maybe she just needed a break from it all, she thought. But just as she was about to head out for a quick walk to freshen her mind and grab a coffee, Jen, her assistant, walked in:

"Don't forget about your 1 p.m. You're interviewing a creative director for the Jackson Aviation account."

"Oh, shoot. OK – on it. Zoom link in the invite?"

"You got it."

"Excited." Yet she wasn't. "Thanks a ton." Yet, Jen was just doing her job.

Stone opened her computer, facing once again the No Place Like Venice email and the opened tabs on Chrome about "When is the right time to start your own business?" Her inbox became a mirror of who she wanted to be, but she never had the guts to go there. She closed all of them with the agility of a hacker, a healthy paranoia she developed ever since meetings became more virtual, and she might be in a sudden position to have to share her screen. She opened the link for the virtual call, where Tyler Bennett awaited. The whitest CD they could hire for the whitest company in the US – Jackson Aviation. That was just the most honest truth, and she hated it – a white company from Kentucky wants an agency that's equitable on paper, but that will have a bright white dude working for the account. Plus, Stone had to balance her presence at the table, as she was already the only woman in that room, and as much as Mr. Jackson respected her, he respected the culture he grew up in more.

"What are you looking for?" Tyler asked.

"I'm looking for passion, for hunger, for curious people. I'm looking for people who are in love with this industry." Stone replied with a serious authoritarian tone.

"Love that."

"I mean, I've been doing this for so long, I wouldn't have stayed in this business if I didn't like my job. I wouldn't stay in this agency if I didn't appreciate the people here."

"Tell me about Daniel Cohen. I've yet to meet him. Would I get to work with him?"

"He's a great partner, a team leader, believes in good work and will push for it. I mean, I wouldn't be here if I didn't admire him."

If the corporate world was a Hollywood movie, Stone would win the Oscar for it, one for each season she played leading actress. Everyone wanted to work with her, to come to the amazing agency she was a part of because she could make even Jackson Aviation sound like an exciting account. She quickly decided she liked Tyler. Years of interviewing helped her determine quickly who was suited for the job, and she always thought an interview was about the questions, not the answers.

"I'm going for a walk for lunch. Call me if the house is burning down," Stone told Jen, who was blasting music in her headphones behind her little cubicle. She nodded to the rhythm of the music, trying to look cool in front of Stone as she was terribly intimidated by her, but Jen's cute little face betrayed a really nice human being, maybe a little too nice for advertising.

New York was beautiful that day, so Stone decided to head to City Hall Park, which was just around the corner from the office. It's incredible how much a bit of fresh air can do for you, particularly in New York. As she turned the corner on Park Row, she bumped into Kate Garcia, one of her best work friends from when she was at Jolie Will, her previous agency. Garcia was a tall, freckled, natural-born, red-haired woman of Iberian descent. Back at Jolie Will, Kate was running the retail business for the agency. Her work-life balance was so poor because of the quick supply deadlines that she never had a chance to take care of herself. That's why Kate's hair was always very long, as she had no time to cut it. Her freckles were always hiding behind dark eye circles, and she was always, alwaaaays carrying a venti latte with her. To everyone who knew her, she was "Fire Latte."

"Stone?"

"Oh my god, Kate, Fire Latte. Wow."

"Fire Matcha," Kate replied as she lifted up a cup of matcha in her hand and laughed.

Stone was speechless. Kate was just returning from a yoga class. Her hair was cut as a long bob and though she just finished off her class, her hair looked annoyingly perfect. The dark circles were gone, and she just seemed – happy.

"How are you, Stone? Still holding up? Still in the trenches?"

"You know it. My birth was…"

"A 60-second ad," Fire Latte interjected, then laughed.

"Yup. Perfect arch narrative," Stone added.

It was their inside joke. Stone's mom delivered her in one of the shortest births ever recorded in Boston, at just shy over 60 seconds of labor. So, naturally, whenever someone asked her why she got into advertising, her answer was that she was born in a 60-second ad. It was short, on camera, and had a happy ending. Thus, her career was inevitable.

"How are you? What have you been up to?" Stone asked.

"I'm out, Stone. Out of advertising. There's more to life than ads," Fire Latte replied with a calm that Stone hasn't seen in years.

"Mhm…"

"I mean, don't listen to me; you know me. I quit Jolie Will one year ago. One day, I just said enough. Enough. Picked up my bag and never returned."

"Good for you. I imagine it was hard to let go."

"I mean, to be honest, I was a little disappointed that no one in the press actually cared to write an article about it, but I mean, there's no dirt. I didn't leave to join another corporation."

"I doubt that's the case; you just managed to keep it under the radar."

"I guess," she replied carelessly.

"So, what have you been doing?" Stone asked, intrigued, perhaps even taking a step closer to her as if she was about to find out a secret.

"The first two months, I slept. So. So. So. Much. Then one day, and you know I wasn't the sporty type, I accidentally passed by this studio called Calm & Alive. It was a beautiful space – part flower shop, part coffee shop, part meditation space. The moment I walked in, I fell in love with it. The smell of roses, coffee, and small air drafts of sweat coming from their hot yoga studio they had upstairs was mesmerizing. I used to go there to read in the mornings, carelessly spending my savings. Slowly, I started to get to know the people there – the owners, waiters, and clients. They were great, but had no idea how to do business or how to sell themselves. So, I offered to help. Long story short, six months later, I became a minority partner and opened a communication studio for wellness companies. I pick the clients. I work to make a living instead of living to work. Yup. There it is. Fire Latte Cliche. Whoop!"

"That's exciting. Place sounds like a dream. Calm & Alive. I'll stop by," Stone replied.

"Oh, definitely. It's just around the corner. Go check it out and tell them you're my friend. I'd come with you, but I gotta run to a meeting."

Stone smiled, but wondered whether it was all as wonderful as she made it sound. Maybe it was because this was her daily routine – pretending to be more excited than she was, more in control than she was, right for the job she was given. Stone couldn't believe the transformation or that she's actually going to a meeting in yoga pants and all sweaty.

"Hey, I'd love to grab drinks sometime," Stone yelled as Fire Latte was already several feet away.

"Love to. Let's do it. Who knows, maybe you can join me," Fire Latte replied while turning around and walking backward, like a kid.

Stone smiled not knowing what to answer.

"I'm just messing with you, Stone. I know you have bigger fish to fry, but let's hang." Fire Latte continued turning around and lifting her hand up in the air waving goodbye.

"Totally. Will text you," Stone whispered, though to her it sounded like she yelled.

Stone watched Fire Latte disappear into the crowd with her yoga mat, skinny legs, and sweat. Off she went to a meeting. Stone was left with that bitter taste of what if, feeding itself on a thread of emails from No Place Like Venice and her dreams of doing her own thing. She reached out for her phone, and it already had five missed calls, 75 unread emails, and 10 texts. First one up: "Tyler Bennett accepted our offer." The HR director texted her. She started to scroll through all the unread messages. Mr. Jackson from Jackson Aviation texted, as did Daniel Cohen, Bobby, and the latest one was from Jen desperately asking her to head back because she was about to miss a review. "What review?" she texted back, sighed, took another sip of her coffee, then sent another one to Jen: "I'll be right there. Tell them to wait for me."

As she walked into the office, she saw the entire creative team gathered in Daniel's office together with Michael.

"What did I miss?" Stone smiled calmly as she walked in.

"I seriously don't understand why we need to have so many reviews. We need time to work," Taylor told Stone loudly as she stepped into the second Amon SLF review of the day, which she also found a waste of time.

"Ah, Stone decided to join us," Michael, the CEO, said as she walked into the office.

"Apologies for that. I was grabbing a coffee."

"That's why you have Jen, don't you?" Michael retorted. Stone smiled, but mentally flipped off him and his bullying.

"Guys, this is going to be quick. I sat down with Michael after our ad gallery review, and we'd like to address some changes by tomorrow a.m. to the work," Daniel said with a smile on this face. To everyone in the room, this sounded like a late night at the office.

"Here's what we love about the work," he continued. "Loving the new experience route, super on brief, disruptive, great, love the acquisition model – but we're not very keen on the women direction."

"You mean SLF identity direction?" Stone pointed out.

"Yeeeaaah. I mean, it's definitely different, but we don't feel like they'll be ready to go there."

"Is it about what they think they should do, or is it about us recommending what's the right thing to do? Aren't they paying us to do the latter?" Stone said.

"Stone, take a chill pill." Michael said and patted Daniel on the back, laughing as if it was their internal joke.

"It's a genuine question. Aren't we tired of just asking clients to take baby steps into category leadership? This is a brand new automotive experience for a brand new type of client. Shouldn't we be more overt about that?"

"I'm not buying it, Stone," Michael added.

"Didn't you say you loved the script in the a.m.?" Stone asked Daniel.

"Come up with a new idea by tomorrow," Michael concluded and stood up. "Danny, let's look at the strategy setup and get the deck ready. Let's let the guys work."

Daniel smiled and complied, pretending they'll be able to solve what the team weren't able to solve in one-and-a-half months.

"Fuck," Stone thought to herself, then smiled at her team with the calm she saw in Fire Latte: "Well, fun times in advertising. We can totally do this. Taylor, Zayan, let's sit together and write scripts while Fernando and Jason start thinking of a different visual identity system."

"Jason's out, Stone," Taylor noted.

"What do you mean? Where is he?"

"Bobby pulled him for a beer project he has to deliver next week."

"Next week?! That's, like, years away."

"Mhmmmmm," Taylor mumbled as she knew that this would piss Stone off, then walked out of the office.

Stone stormed into Bobby's office, but it was already late, and he already had left for the day. By 6.30 p.m., Bobby was always out of the office, which was odd by all New York corporate life standards. That drove Stone mad, but whom could she complain about this to in an era where so much importance is being placed on work-life balance? He chose balance.

His office still smelled like his expensive oaky cologne, meaning he probably just left, so Stone stormed out toward the elevator to see whether she could catch him. The open space was still filled with creative folks nodding their heads to the music blasting in their headphones, creating a unique rhythm of nervous keyboard typing and mouse clicks, typical of corporate living. In the middle of it all, Stone was literally running to catch Bobby, but unlike in a happy ending, when she turned the corner, Bobby wasn't there. "Shit," she thought as she barely caught her breath. She picked up the phone and called Daniel to ask for some help, to no avail, as he wasn't answering either.

"Pattrick texted me. He invited us for dinner at Rasputin at 8.30. Can you make it?" her husband texted.

Stone was infuriated. She had been neglecting her marriage for the past couple of months. They've had plenty of ups and downs, and there's only so much her husband will take.

"I can't make it, babe. Michael just killed one of our directions."

"OK."

"Are you going though?"

"Yes."

Her husband was just the right amount of telegraphic for her to know he's mad.

"Good. Have fun."

He never texted back, and the fear of missing out was now starting to bubble up inside Stone. The corporate part of her identity is starting to fade away. All she really wanted these days was to cuddle up with her husband in a blanket and watch Netflix, but she can't, and nobody really cares. She was a victim of her own making, a race she's been running for the past 15 years with no finish line in sight. That's the worst kind, she always thought. To keep running without knowing when the race is going to end, without the joy of actually passing the finish line.

"You OK, Stone?" Taylor asked as Stone almost bumped into her.

"Oh hey, Taylor. Yeah – emails."

"So, what's the status?"

"What do you mean?"

"Jason?"

"What about Jason?"

"Is he back on the project?"

"Oh, yeah, no he's not. I can't reach Bobby. Tell Fernando he'll have to run it. Let's meet back in two hours and see where we stand. I'll start writing some ideas now too."

"OK," Taylor said, then walked away mumbling.

***

With the pitch 24 hours away, Stone was resigned to the idea that they'll just go in with one creative direction. Everything her and her team created in the past day was nowhere near the level of thinking they had up until Michael tore down her favorite direction in the ad gallery postmortem. She watched Michael making gestures of disappointment about this in Daniel's office, as Daniel tried to cool him down, but from her perspective, she was too tired to react anymore. They can fire her for all she cared at this point, to be honest. They'd be doing her a favor. She was at that point in the process when things just start to crumble within you. All the years you put into the work, all the enthusiasm that you had when you started, all the love for the work you do disappear. All you want is silence, all you want is a break, all you want is to be able to hear your thoughts and kiss your loved ones. At this point, you also start doubting the work, even though you seem like the biggest cheerleader in the world.

As she watched them arguing like in a silent movie, she opened her email, and there, on top of her inbox, pinned, was the email from *FW* magazine again. The irony. She opened the questions sent by the magazine to help her prep for the live interview coming up in a few days.

First question: "What does a day in your life look like?"

"Disastrous," Stone thought.

Second question: "What's the biggest challenge for a woman in your position?"

"Where do I start? Men, depression, having to do twice the work so I can have a job and a family," she continued with her inner dialogue.

"Hey, Stone," Daniel interrupted her invisible interview, "what are you up to?"

"Nothing, just catching up with emails. What's up?" she replied, emotionless.

"I chatted with Michael. He's OK with us just going in with one direction; we feel confident you aren't going to lose the pitch for us."

"Sounds good, Daniel." Stone smiled and nodded as an acceptance of maybe the biggest passive-aggressive statement she heard in years, making her fully accountable for the outcome.

It was in that moment that she thought it's time to take a *corporatebbatical*, or whatever you want to call it – a year during which she'd focus only on her plans, dreams, and ideals. A sabbatical at her level is perhaps one of the most difficult decisions she could make. Even though dreaming about hitting "send" to an email with this bold decision was entertaining, it wasn't the decision for her. After all, she had big career dreams, and to be honest, not a big enough safety net to support her lavish lifestyle. She wasn't about to jump on the quitting wagon the industry has been faced with in the past few years. She wasn't a quitter, nor was she that brave.

She opened the creative presentation for the pitch one more time and started taking notes on things to say and how to strategize to ensure they buy the idea and don't question why they came with only one. Rehearsing what to say always came in handy for her. Michael also always insisted they rehearse before a big presentation as a group, to time things right, say things right, and make things right. Sometimes, it made sense – other times, it was just a ridiculous circus they had to do because corporations are rigid, and their processes are old. This time, though, even Stone admitted it made sense, but she hated the idea that Michael believes going with just one idea that was bold enough already seemed like defeat. She thought that as a leader, he wasn't brave enough, that he just wanted to check boxes and get his annual bonus. She thought he had no leadership skills, didn't know half of his department's names, and at times even forgot what Stone's first name was anyway. On the other hand, there's also the possibility that the idea and the work behind it were just – bad. Come to think of it, just like an artist being anxious about her own art before a show, or like a public speaker thinking she won't remember a single word from her well-written speech, Stone also felt this way about the work she did in the past month and a half.

By this time, Stone felt like her body was giving up on her. Exhaustion is sneaky. You don't feel it. It's like a silent painful drip from within. The first days you start to feel it, you manage to push through, and slowly you stop feeling it. Feeling drowsy or dizzy and needing a lot of coffee become part of your life, so you think you feel fine, but slowly, slowly, you start degrading. That's where Stone was headed. She was, pun intended, pretty stoned on exhaustion.

In 24 hours, she would give a presentation for maybe the biggest pitch of her career, against Velocity 5, against that guy playing Candy Crush next to her on the plane – who, by the way, probably was making three times what she was, so good for him and his mobile phone skills.

Stone had no idea how to write notes and talking points for a presentation. She always saw others holding little pieces of paper that they would look at for, like, three seconds and know immediately what they should be talking about. However, Stone wrote entire chapters and sagas instead of notes. The only way she could look at those little papers in a few seconds and know what's she's supposed to be saying was if she had binoculars instead of glasses and could read at the speed of light. Instead of just writing three words or main ideas, she wrote entire phrases in bad doctor-like handwriting that was so messy, she barely could understand it herself. Taking notes for her wasn't really an option, so she developed a special skill to improvise her way through presentations, be entertaining, and sell with her heart, rather than with a perfectly staged presentation.

She was now entering the panic stage – panicked that the work wasn't good, that she had no idea why she pushed for this idea, that she was incapable of actually selling the work, and that she'd get fired.

Panic was the middle name of advertising executives for years. It's what they lived on. It was their drug. It wasn't cocaine, like in the '70s, or late-night whisky. Nope. Panic was the drug. Anxiety was the proof that you did corporate work right. Exhaustion was a testimony to devotion. For some, it all stopped there. For others who were more unlucky, things sometimes would go sideways. Just like with cocaine, whisky, or any other vice known to man. Exhaustion, just like any vice, turned out to be deadly for some.

That night, Stone went home early. It was barely 8 p.m. when she hugged her husband good night. She was in so much need of a hug, a kiss, and some sex. Unfortunately, she fell asleep before she could even get to second base. "Is it really that pathetic how 35-year-olds are today?"she thought many times. "If we fall flat at this age, what the hell are we gonna do when we're 60?" However, she was one of the lucky ones. Her husband really understood her career. He was a great supporter, and he never complained about a thing. Sometimes she'd stop and wonder whether this was all real. Sure, he opposed many proposed changes to her career that would affect them both, but the daily stuff never bothered him. Their lifestyle never bothered him. She was really lucky – or at least that's what it seemed. What you don't know can't hurt you, right? She was too busy to know anyway. Truth is, if your love life is OK, your career will want to take over, and as it takes over, it'll want more and more. It'll want domination – a life dedicated just to it, without anyone else being part of it. Careers are like a needy mistress. No wonder the highest rates of divorce are among very successful people.

That night, she fell asleep during an NBA game David was watching. Arguably, a lot of women would, but in her case, she really loved the NBA. Maybe because that was the only sport she was good at when she was young. Between the whistles, cheers, and excited commentators, she fell asleep and woke up at dawn, drooling on the leather pillow. Not a very pretty picture, but hey, in reality, men won't carry you in their arms and tuck you into bed. That was reserved for the Mr. Bigs and Cinderella-esque movies. In Manhattan, you carry yourself. Pick yourself up and carry on, woman!

It was 5 a.m., and life wasn't looking particularly great. Stone woke up, looked at her watch, and realized she's very close to losing her 7.30 a.m. flight from La Guardia to San Diego. However, never underestimate a corporate woman's ability to suit up, pack up, and leave the house in 30 minutes. Stone was a travel ninja.

As she boarded the plane with Anderson and his minions, she had a flashback of Fire Latte – how radiant and peaceful she looked, and how fit she got. Was this all worth it? She shook her head, realizing it's really not the time to doubt her career path and decided to let tomorrow's Stone worry about that.

When they landed in San Diego, it was raining. Like, seriously, when does it ever rain in San Diego? As they got out of the airport, a long line at the taxis looked very discouraging for what was ahead of them. Stone looked around and didn't spot any trace of the Velocity 5 team, so they must have had the meeting the day before, she thought.

"I think we're the last ones, Anderson."

"It could be good for us, though," Anderson reassured her. She nodded in agreement.

Presenting the last pitch could be good for them, but presenting just one idea may look like underdelivering. They didn't have a chance to set the tone around being decisive, bold, and having a point of view, and Velocity 5 most likely already charmed them with their accolades. So, as she walked into the conference room at Amon's headquarters, she already thought of how she could swing her audience.

Even though it was empty and quiet, the meeting room was big and intimidating, like a concert hall in the absence of a concert. It scares you a bit and comes along with flutters of butterflies in your stomach. Anderson's minions suddenly started to pull a bunch of crazy pitch artillery out of their bags – name tents, agendas with their agency logo on it, pens, pencils, papers, and big boards with storyboards and visuals. Stone couldn't tell where all these came from; they all had carry-ons. The minions were performing a show of corporate magic, their own version of an advertising *Extreme Makeover* that easily could run on HGTV. And just like that, the room was set up for success.

"You should sit there, Stone. Across from Peter," Anderson said.

"Are you sitting next to him?"

"Yes. Michael sits here, and Danny here," Anderson continued, but Stone stopped listening at that point.

There's certainly nothing new about that pitch theater, and all the other agencies surely played a similar scheme – creative on one side, client service on the other side, power players next to decision makers – as if the clients couldn't tell what they were doing. However silly it was, though, Stone was a team player and believed in their game.

When Peter Amon walked into the room, the universe went into complete silence. All the trivial conversations about the weather, holidays, and different children of people they just met went mute as if a button was pushed. He smiled warmly, nodded to everyone, and sat down, calmly arranging his agenda and pen while acknowledging they were now ready to start.

"Good morning, Mr. Amon. We can't tell you how excited we are to be here with you today." Anderson started the meeting, and with it came the great corporate choreography of smiles and nodding heads, "I must tell you, we had so much fun working on this brief."

"Err, not so much," Stone thought.

"The possibility of changing the automotive industry – to push it forward and revolutionize how we travel and live – isn't something we come across daily in our advertising world. So, thank you for giving us a chance to show you what we can do for your business. Today, in the room with me are Michael Brown, our CEO; Daniel Cohen, our amazing visionary; and one of the most creative minds of our century, our rare and precious Stone," Anderson then laughed, proud of making a mediocre pun, then continued "whom you've met already in the debriefing session, and Steve, Courtney and Lewis, our account executives for new businesses."

"Welcome, everyone. Nice to meet you," Peter Amon said, saluting candidly.

"Let's get down to business," Anderson said as he flipped through the presentation slides projected on the big screen in the conference room.

The next 20 slides of charts, graphs, and accolades were all fuzzy to Stone. She was getting into the groove. While looking at her notes, written as long as chapters, and trying to figure out what she wanted to say, she suddenly felt like all the practice, all the weeks spent doing the work, all of it was gone. Her mind was completely blank. After 15 years, she still had stage fright.

"And I'll pass it over to Stone to walk you through the work," Anderson suddenly said, catapulting Stone out of her stage fright zone all the way to the middle of the pitch stage. As if awakening from a dream, Stone stood up and headed toward the screen in the middle of the room. All eyes were on her. She could only feel Peter Amon's stare and his serious demeanor, already a little bored from the slides of self-appreciation they'd just presented. As she arrived in front of the screen, she stopped, took a mental breath, then started speaking. Suddenly, all that stress magically vanished, and every word and sentence made sense, as if Anderson's minions whipped up corporate spells to help her out.

"Peter," She opened her creative pleading with a bit of hesitancy, as she always did when trying to look casual, but doing it with one of the most powerful men in the state of California. "Amon Automobiles is a pioneer. Everybody knows that. You entered the market almost out of nowhere and shook it to its foundation. Now you're sizing up how the industry should look like in the future. Sure, others are in the game too, but you're doing it boldly, placing a bet on disruption. And in this context, you need an agency that's ready to do the same. We aren't standing here in front of you today to show you options, we aren't here to show you pathways you can take. We're here to show you just one way because it's the only way in. You need an agency that's ready to take the risks with you and consult you on the best way forward. Because when you're wearing pioneer shoes, you can't stop at every step to figure out the next one. So, today, Peter, you're only going to see one idea from us. THE idea that Amon SLF needs to become THE leader for years to come in the autonomous car industry."

Peter Amon stood there, poker-faced, waiting for the next slide.

"And that idea is SLF Identity." Stone paused for two seconds. She always did that to catch up on any body language from her audience, but Peter Amon was smarter than that and gave nothing away to blow his cover. Thus, she continued. "When the entire category is talking about autonomous driving, Amon SLF will be talking about the experience that any car should have in the 21st century. Autonomy is a given, so let's talk about what else. Let's talk about the safety, comfort, and freedom to move at your own pace. But let's talk about it only with a select few, carefully picked consumers based on our audience segments and make the car even more desirable. This will refocus the conversation from autonomy and ethics of self-driving cars to the lifestyle that can come with it, to the car that can finally reflect who you are. And whoever isn't ready for that lifestyle should probably stay out of it anyway. It's bold, and people will say we're crazy, but that's what pioneers do."

Peter smiled for a fraction of a second as Stone finished her opening statement. That's when Stone knew she won the pitch. Slide after slide, Stone was flying. She had Peter Amon eating out of the palm of her hand with every word, every headline, every narrative she went through. Finally, Stone realized the power she held in her hands and why meritocracy never can be diminished by any social circumstance that may come with the times. As she finished the presentation, everyone was smiling. Peter Amon stood up, walked up to Stone, and shook her hand – and her hand only – before leaving the room: "Great job. We'll be in touch."

As the room cleared out, and it was just her agency in the room, she felt as if a stone were lifted off her chest. Life was fun again, people were nice again, and that mountain of stress was now gone.

She looked at Daniel and Michael, and smiled, expecting them to say something to her. Michael smiled back and suddenly yelled: "Fucking amazing, Danny. You did it again."

"Thanks, man," Danny replied. "Being bold and going in with just one idea paid off."

"Gotta go, need to catch a flight to Louisville," Michael said, then packed his bag in a split second.

"Heading to Jackson Aviation?"

"You betcha. Jackson wants to talk, so gotta go charm him."

"Good luck, man." Daniel then waved goodbye.

"Thanks. Hey, Stone, good job," Michael told Stone briefly as he rushed out of the room.

Stone just stood there and watched the room dynamics in disbelief. It was boys town all over again. As she packed her stuff, she saw a text from her husband: "You'll kill it. I trust you." She smiled. Apparently, everyone who wasn't working with her believed in her, and those who did couldn't care less. Maybe it was all Daniel's credit that we had a good outcome. Maybe if he hadn't decided to allow her to go with just one direction, they wouldn't have won it. However, she was the one who strategized what to say and argued for it. He said nothing. He stood there for two hours and said nothing. All he did was say stuff like, "I love this, Peter," as if Peter cared what Daniel liked.

As their van pulled in front of Amon Automobiles, she saw another van just coming in. Was it Velocity 5? Did they not present yet? Were they not the last pitch after all? Did they just blow her strategy? Stone's breath stopped for a beat or two.

"Stone, you coming?" Daniel shouted from the inside of the van.

"Yeah, now," she replied, while waiting to see who got out of the van.

The door of the other van opened, and suddenly a group of engineering students came out to tour the facility. She sighed with relief and got in the van to head back to New York.

On the plane, she spotted the Candy Crush guy. She was right after all. They did have a meeting with Amon before them. It must have been the day before in the afternoon, so they must have been the second agency to present, which is never a good thing. She nodded her head as a sign of salutation to the Candy Crush guy, sat down, and pressed play to listen to Sia again.

During the entire flight back to New York, she thought about Fire Latte – how great she looked and how glowing and brave she was. Was it time for her to look the same? She kept pushing it back for years, promising herself she'd do it eventually. She'll go on her own, build a company, and start over. But how should she do it? Should she do it with a bang? Should it be a middle finger? Will anyone care anyway? Somehow even forgetting that she was chosen as one of the top five businesswomen in New York, she still wondered whether anyone actually cared about what she did with her career. She opened her notes on the phone and started writing a wishful letter of resignation. She used to do this quite a lot. It was a writer's way of venting.

"Dear friends, I've decided to say stop for a while. Maybe a couple of months, maybe a year, who knows. I feel like I don't identify anymore with how we do business. We've become this place where people go to see their life pass by in endless meetings and great ideas grow into mediocrity. They often end up in a bus shelter waiting, hoping, that someone finally notices it, that they can go up in the world, like on a Times Square billboard, where they can look up and say "I've made it!" But nobody ever notices them because they're just plain mediocre. They're one of many.

I've decided to say stop to this for a while. Perhaps it's the single craziest thing I've ever done. I'm working with an amazing bunch of people, earning great pay, and yet it's not enough. I've become tired having to report every move and decision I make or having to ask permission to do what's right. It's like having a full-grown adult asking his mom if he can kiss that girl he likes.

So, I've decided to take a corporatebbatical, a pause from the corporate world. A year where I don't travel the world, or perhaps I do, but just a little bit. A year where I invest in my ideas, my projects, my company. And see where it leads. It could lead back to that billboard in Times Square, or it could lead to new heights.

I'm putting all my savings on the line, saying a prayer, and I'll see you all in a year."

She closed her computer right as the flight started to descend into New York City. Could this be how she leaves the industry – with a bang? Could she do it? Take a corporate sabbatical and do her own thing? Will she have the guts that Fire Latte had?

When she got home, her husband was cooking dinner for them.

"Truffle carbonara for the winner!" He yelled from the kitchen.

"Don't jinx it!" She yelled back.

"Leave all your belongings at the door – that includes your phone, especially your phone, and come here."

Stone smiled. Her life was finally back to a little normal. It was that feeling she felt after each pitch. As she took her phone out of her bag to leave it on the counter, she saw a text from Mr. Jackson at Jackson Aviation.

"Babe?"

"Coming." she opened the text anxiously, as if that stone was back on her chest keeping her from breathing.

"Ms. Stone, I'm sorry you didn't fly into Louisville today. I told Michael as well. I'm thrilled with the work Tyler has been doing on the account. We just got test results back – they're our best ones yet. Great job. Thank you for the partnership."

"I told you we'll fly, Mr. Jackson," she texted back, then smiled.

As she stepped into the kitchen and gave her husband a big hug, going solo started to feel better than ever. Was she emotional? Maybe. But with these kinds of decisions, how can you not be? People underestimate the importance of emotions in business. We're all made of emotions, so you can't just pretend we're acting like machines.

She looked at her husband and knew that he won't support her decision – not because he didn't trust her, not because he couldn't support her – but because he knew how insecure she'll get. After all, this was her decision to make and hers only. She wanted what Fire Latte had, even if it puts her career on the line.

After she took her first bite of truffle carbonara, then kissed her husband, and as they finally made love later after two months of her work ordeal, all of it made sense. She needed a break. Impulsively, without thinking twice, she opened her computer, pulled up the note she jotted on the plane, and added one more line.

"Consider this a notice of resignation. My last day will be August 1."

Enter.

Chapter 3

Coco

When Coco was in high school, she daydreamed about love, about meeting that charming man who will be kind to her, love her, and want to have nobody else but her. However, her high school years never give you what you're looking for.

Coming from a place of insecurity, maybe like most girls at that age, she desperately wanted to be with somebody. Thus, in the quest to find that somebody, she felt like she should just give all men a try, so she became promiscuous. She started to hang out in dubious entourages, yet managed to remain a virgin until she was 18. Hard to believe considering who her friends were and what they were up to.

She dated old men, weird men, hot shot men, mean men, and bad men. She dated all men, but she never dated nice men. Actually, every time she dated a nice man, she felt as if something was wrong. They felt boring and too uncomplicated for her, as there was nothing for her to figure out or rescue. For some reason, she never found that she was good enough to have somebody good.

If you ask her about it today, she still remembers this one guy who, on his first date with her, was so excited about who she was and whom she looked like that he called all his friends to brag about dating his own Keira Knightley. And it all happened in front of her eyes, as if his lame grandeur was supposed to be some sort of compliment to her. So, she dumped him and never returned his calls again.

She once saw a movie in which friends were discussing the number of partners they had sex with, and Coco, just like any woman who saw that movie, thought of hers. What was her number? She couldn't remember precisely, no matter how many times she tried. She just couldn't get it right. I mean, don't get me wrong, she didn't date just three guys all her life, but rather a few dozen – though not in the hundreds. She wasn't a sexual predator, just very undecided, and because of that, her brain blocked out some of them, as if she was ashamed of her past and the men in it. Except for some. Some of them couldn't be forgotten. Like the time she finally had sex with a man she was obsessed with, but whose last name she never knew.

Or like the time she ended up with a man way older than her in a hotel room, but instead of having sex, they ended up playing chess all night. But perhaps the one time she'll never forget, and there's a reason why that time of her life is locked in a locker somewhere hidden, was when she was almost raped and killed by two guys who were friends of friends. You'd think these things don't happen to people around you, to just anyone, to people who don't get into strangers' cars or hitchhike in the middle of nowhere, but if you ask the Coco of today, she'd tell you it doesn't happen to you until somehow it does. If you could see the Coco of today, you wouldn't believe something like this could have happened to her.

She was in her senior year of high school and was trying to get home from a party at a friend's lake house. Two guys, best buds of Chloe's boyfriend at the time, offered to drive her up. Not only did everyone know them, but she also happened to like one of them, so she thought she just hit the jackpot and might end up with a date tomorrow. Yet, high school years never give you what you're looking for. They were just a few minutes into the drive when they suddenly turned right onto a forest road. A few feet down the road, Jack, one of the guys, hit the brakes, and the car stopped in the middle of nowhere. He rolled the window down and lit up a joint. She rolled down her window, as she couldn't stand the smell of burnt weed. It was pitch dark and extremely quiet, so much so that you could still hear the echo from the music at the party on the other side of the lake.

"What are we doing here?" asked Coco, but got no reply.

Jack took another hit from the joint, looked at Larry, who smiled, then looked back at Coco. Suddenly, Jack opened the door, got out of the car, and opened Coco's door:

"Take your clothes off," he demanded.

"What?" Coco asked in disbelief.

"You heard him, bitch," Larry yelled from the front seat, anxious and angry like a crazy man.

"Take your clothes off now. Don't make me say it again," Jack repeated with a menacingly calm, slow tone.

"What? No? Are you crazy? What's wrong with you?" she screamed, closing the door in front of Jack. Angry, he opened it, grabbed her by the shirt, and threw her onto the wet muddy ground in the forest.

"Clothes on the ground or body in the lake," he now screamed at her.

Coco was lying there in disbelief, when suddenly she heard the door from the other side and saw Larry's boots running over to Jack's side. He stopped, looked at her, then at Jack, who was completely transformed into a madman, then suddenly he dragged her up by grabbing her ponytail and pushed her into the back of the car. Coco cried for help, but in the middle of nowhere, no one could hear her. He pushed her belly in the back of the car and her head in front so her butt would push back. She could hear a zipper.

"Wait, I have an idea," Jack screamed at Larry.

Jack pushed Coco on her side and opened the trunk. For a second, she didn't know whether avoiding rape from Larry was better than what was about to happen. Larry then put her inside the trunk and laughed as he slammed the door shut. While lying in that small, dark space, all she could hear was their indistinct mumbling and laughing. Suddenly, she heard footsteps heading toward the front of the car. They got in and turned on the engine. The car started to move, and they drove fast and faster, turning around with rapid moves and drifting, throwing Coco from one side of the trunk to the other as if she was a potato bag. As she bruised and thought she'd never see the light of day again, she suffered through their laughing, as she didn't see the end of this. In that moment, Coco had her first real conversation with God.

Perhaps it was divine intervention or the modern miracles of sobering up, but after a few minutes of driving around like crazy, the car suddenly stopped. Jack stepped outside, opened the trunk, dragged her out and threw her on the ground. She thought she heard him whisper, "Run!" so she did. The car took off, and the taillights disappeared in the distance on the forest road. Coco found herself bruised and hurting in the middle of the forest in the dead of night, which by all accounts was terrifying, but in that moment, it all seemed serene. Her well-being finally was back in her hands, and all she had to do was walk home and not tell a single soul what happened. Nobody needed to know. She's OK. This would ruin her if anyone ever knew what happened.

Back then, there was no Me Too Movement, no education about how having sex with someone underaged was illegal, and her parents never told her that something like this could happen and that she didn't want the entire high school calling her a slut. In her mind, she asked for it; otherwise, why did she get in the car with the two guys? So, she never told anyone and was just thankful nothing worse happened. She licked her wounds and carried on, thinking the scar would heal itself, rather than become a big thick keloid.

As an adult, she left that life behind, grew up, and made a name for herself by running as far away as possible. With this came a whole different set of problems. She learned that a relationship takes more than just lying down and spreading your legs; it takes work, attention, and care. However, she never was exposed to any of this, nor focused on acquiring any special wife skills. Perhaps because she had a turbulent dating past, she always desired financial independence and wanted to become someone in life. Unfortunately for her, and contrary to what most women hoped for, men weren't interested in her financial independence or professional accomplishments. They weren't dating her career, bank account, or the name she made for herself. Perhaps that's exactly why the man she ended up with called her Coco, though obviously, that wasn't her true full name. In return, she sometimes called him Davey.

Davey was a notorious serial dater. He probably dated all the women from his home town and a considerable number of ladies from the posh New York bar scene. Davey had all the things bad boys have and nice guys don't, so Coco naturally fell in love with him in an instant. She felt constantly anxious around him – anxious that she wasn't good enough for him, not as pretty as the other women he had dated, not woman enough to meet his serious relationship needs, and not dependent enough to avoid threatening him intellectually. And it was weird because by all measures, she looked good – relatively tall, skinny, and genetically programmed to stay that way, with sensual lines and a sculptured face. Maybe it just happened that anxiety took over. She always felt like he'd leave her, and it was perhaps the first time in all her relationships when she had abandonment issues. If all relationships are something to work on, hers went above and beyond.

When they first met, it was electric. She had that fire in her belly that she thought she'd never feel again as a grown 30-year-old woman. But she did. She felt anxious every time she met him and felt overjoyed when he called her. And he did call her, again and again, until it became a relationship. She had become accustomed to men running away from her and always wondered whether it was because maybe she was frigid, maybe because she had made a career for herself, or maybe it was her family. Somehow, over the years, many men wouldn't last beyond the third date. However, Davey was a different breed. He kept calling, kept showing up, and wasn't intimidated.

She dated a lot of guys in her life, but she had only been in two long-term serious relationships before. She had this premonition, this karmic conception that the third relationship is the one that eventually would lead to marriage. She became somewhat obsessed with that number, so when electricity fired up in her belly upon meeting Davey, she knew he may be her number three, or maybe she just wanted him to be the one.

Their early dates were spoiled with champagne and a lot of time spent together. She actually ended up spending the night at his place from day one, which wasn't necessarily unnatural for Coco, but she liked to think that he was special because it started that way. The more they got to know each other and realized they had common friends, the closer they got. For him, she was that calm feeling he needed. For her, he was the fire her inner introvert craved. She wanted a man who would run her life and have mad sex with her. She wanted full domination – not in a sexual or abusive way, but someone who was confident enough to tell her when she was dead wrong. She always thought that she craved that because she was running an entire department in her professional life and always had to be the one who made decisions. In fact, the reason why she probably craved domination was because she had bits of unresolved issues with her absent, yet dominant, father.

Now in her adult life, Coco learned to understand that you can read all the books you want, but no inspirational Socrates or Mark Twain quote can get you out of the trouble you put yourself in.

Her mom married a dominant man. Coco's dad had terrible mood swings, and you sometimes could feel it just from the way his feet would touch the ground, his looks, and his energy. He didn't hide it when he had a bad day, and everyone in the family was about to feel his pain as if they were to blame for it. She despised her dad and always dreamed of a dad whom she could talk to, turn to for advice, or go to baseball games with – a dad who would cheer from the crowd at her high school graduation. But he was none of that and never made it to any celebration, including her graduation. He didn't kiss her proudly when she left for her prom, have a conversation with her first boyfriend, give her advice about her career, or teach her anything. He was absent. Her dad loved her, in theory, but loved himself more.

Then there's Davey, who was a bit like her dad – jumpy at times, unpredictable, very self-centered, and had a lot of other traits she had seen in her childhood before. Silently, without her consent, Coco had become the definition of "daddy issues."

As the years passed, Davey and Coco started to morph into one another. Coco became more jumpy, and Davey became more calm around her. She transformed into this possessive, jealous woman who on the outside seemed careless, flexible, and open to open relationships. On the inside, though, she was jealous and possessive. The balance had swung the other way. In reality and by all beauty standards, she had nothing to worry about – she looked good, was super successful, was financially independent, and was better than all the other women he had dated on any scale. And yet, she was now the complete opposite of the calm Davey whom she initially started dating. It was as if he transformed her.

Now, let's not blame it all on Davey, who had a lot of flaws, but he also had a couple of very good qualities to even things out. Unlike any man she ever dated, he didn't just support her career, but was proud and super vocal about it. They liked hanging out in the same places and spending money on posh experiences, unlike all the losers she dated before. They liked the same people and holidays, worked hard, and partied hard. When they fought, they really fought. They had the kind of fights you'd see drunk people have in a club and think, like, "Man, they're so drunk. I can't believe they're fighting over this." They fought over stupid things, like forgetting a sweater in a bar, missing an exit on a highway, or forgetting to buy milk. They agreed on everything else in life except, perhaps, babies. Baby conversations were a different league, but let's put that aside for now.

Davey worked on Wall Street – a bit too much of a cliché for Coco, but he was the old school kind of broker. He mocked the start-up bros or the hedgies who only talked about their latest Patek or the model they just fucked. He was passionate about art, old vinyl albums, and luxury linens. He had an artistic side that his overachieving parents never let him nurture. His parents were in finance too and wanted him to follow in their footsteps. In theory, just like Coco, Davey was perfect. He was a smooth talker and a great salesman who could convince anybody of virtually anything he wanted. This sometimes made Coco wonder whether the decisions she had made in the past few years were actually hers, or were they all products of Davey's perfected persuasive techniques? He knew exactly what to say and when to say it, and how to read other people's hesitations or desires, even if he had just met them. So, of course, he didn't have to persuade Coco too much into saying, "I do."

Their marriage was everything Coco dreamed of – a beautiful beachfront ceremony in early September in the Hamptons, followed by an elegant dinner at Blue Swan resort and spa that half of Wall Street attended, then a first class flight to Dubrovnik in Croatia, a place Davey always wanted to visit.

Six years into their relationship, things still were going smoothly. Davey inspired Coco to hustle in her corporate job, teaching her the importance of networking. In return, Davey got financial independence and maturity from Coco, which was something he rarely got from past relationships. Or at least that's what Coco thought she was giving to Davey. They say love fades away, but lately, Davey had become more loving than he used to be, more careful than she had been used to. He'd bring her flowers when he came home from work, pay close attention to all the things she wanted, and whenever he came home late at night from work, he slept on the couch so as not to wake her up. Coco was a light sleeper, and he respected that. Sure, coming home late from work wasn't a common occurrence for Davey, but the night before that morning, though, he did.

Coco woke up very early that one morning, as she had to prep for a busy workday. As she opened her eyes and looked to her right, she realized Davey wasn't there. She rushed down to the living room hoping Davey was there on the couch, asleep as he always is when he comes home late from work. Not surprisingly, he was there, sound asleep, with his tie still on. Coco smiled, gave him a kiss on his forehead, picked up his wallet from the floor, which fell from his pocket, and his phone, which fell screen down on the marble floors. Coco picked it up fearing the screen was cracked, and Davey would be so mad about it, but it wasn't. She smiled thinking how lucky Davey is all the time. He could drop it from a 10-story building, and it still would be OK. As she turned the screen on, though, it lit up. On it were seven unread messages received at 2 a.m. "What time did he get in?" she thought. This was strange. She had a strict policy about not going into other people's phones, but he was her husband, and no matter how emotionally stable you are, no matter how self-confident, no matter how much you love the man, when your gut feeling tells you something's wrong, it's never wrong. There's not enough scientific research on women's gut feelings. Coco's heart started to race at 180 bpm, and as she typed in his password, she knew something wasn't right. Soon, staring at her were seven messages from a Rebbekah Levy. They had been texting for days, possibly weeks. Coco couldn't read them all because as she scrolled through the messages, she got sick to her stomach. She looked at Davey, left the phone on the ground where she found it, and went to shower. She was numb. She didn't cry, scream, or hit the wall. She was numb. She got dressed and ready to go to work. Before she left the house, she approached Davey and kissed him on the forehead like she always did, but this time, she didn't say goodbye. Instead, she said, "Tell Rebbekah I said hi." Davey got up instantly, not knowing exactly what was going on, and as he started asking Coco what she was talking about, Coco slammed the door and left for her meeting without a word. Those five words made it all real for her.

If you've ever been cheated on, you're probably familiar with the cheated heart thudding. It's the strongest thud your heart will make, and it goes on and on and on, vibrating from your chest to your head, from your head to your ears, from your ears to your hands, and all you want is to punch something to set it free. In just a few minutes coming down the elevator from the 48th floor, their relationship flashed in Coco's head, and she couldn't make sense of what just happened. His infidelity made no sense. All those cliches about how people never change were true. Despite her illusions, Davey never changed – he was a serial dater even while in a relationship, more so when married. Was it that he didn't care about her, or was it because she always was working, so like all the other men in her life, he silently quit her? Was this his cue to put in his resignation? Davey didn't just cheat on her; he cheated on her romantic ideal. He cheated on what she believed a relationship should be, or what she wanted them to achieve as a couple. To her, Davey was her best friend, lover, confidant, career counselor, and husband. But as it turned out, she wasn't the same to him. At this point, Coco had no idea what she even meant to Davey. He kept calling and calling, but Coco couldn't bear the idea of hearing his voice.

"Pick up the phone – let's talk," Davey messaged her eventually, as the elevator doors opened. Coco stared at the text for several minutes, but still was numb. She couldn't pick up or text back. If he was so distressed about losing her, why didn't he just run after her and catch her in the lobby, exhausted and sweaty from running down 1,000 stairs? Staring at that guilty text from Davey, she started texting back.

"There's nothing to t...," she wrote, then deleted it and started again.

"I don't know who you are. I don't kn...," then she deleted it again.

"How could you do th..." was her last try, but her fingers stopped typing, and she completely shut down her phone. She didn't want to see any message, any notification, anything going through. She stood still in the lobby of their building, the entrance to their home for the past six years, in the heart of Dumbo, staring at Manhattan. Now their home was crumbling to pieces.

"You thought you could have it all," she told herself as she wiped away tears. "This is the price you pay, you fucking moron."

Somehow, she'd come to believe that everything wrong with their relationship was her fault because she dared to want a career and work for her dreams, and as a consequence, she perhaps ignored her home life.

There's something daunting about infidelity in the times we live in – it strips you of your self-identity. Before, when marriage was a more economic institution, when you'd marry out of economic convenience, not out of love, people would look for romance outside of their relationships. So, infidelity, though taboo since the beginning of modern times, was better accepted – particularly male infidelity. Today, when you're in a relationship out of love, an affair doesn't offer up romance, but rather feeds into curiosity, and in the process ruins relationships. To make matters worse, infidelity today is graphic, raw, and visual, serving up details you never asked for in simple text, selfies, or emails. What goes down during an affair never just stays in that affair.

As she was waiting at the traffic light, she remembered that her aunt also caught her husband cheating and wasn't afraid to talk about it. Unlike Coco, she was an extrovert, a very vocal and busty woman who loved to smoke, and by the time Coco grew up had married three times. But how her aunt found out about the affair was minimal compared with what women today are exposed to. Back then, a little note in her husband's pocket saying, "Can't wait to see you again!" with a red lipstick mark on it and a bit of Chanel sprinkled on the note was all she saw. That's how infidelity operated in those days: part cliche, part imagination. Back then, you had the option of folding your infatuation onto a piece of paper, hiding it, or burning it, pretend like it never happened and know it in your broken heart that you've done everything so that your husband never does it again. But now, everything is stored in the cloud, and every trace of infidelity remains on a server somewhere forever, piling up unmet needs and dreams from different couples everywhere, polluting your mind and the planet.

Today, Coco found out about her partner's infidelity from vivid descriptions of a night and the days that followed, exchanges of pictures, and promises of further dates with Rebbekah Levy. Today, infidelity is more graphic, so it's way more difficult to let it go, move on, forgive, but not forget, etc.

"Mooooove, bitch!" yelled the guy in the car behind her as soon as the traffic light turned green.

Coco was still there, unmovable, contemplating the evolution of infidelity in the 21st century. She was in no condition to drive, but was on autopilot, and routine was the only thing that kept her on track as she was staring into the abyss of insanity. Somehow, she managed to get to her office, and as she arrived at the underground parking garage of her office building, she was numb again. She just stopped in the middle of the parking lot and stared at the water dripping from the faulty air conditioning pipe above, ignoring the valet sitting right next to her window to pick up her key. What's next from here? will her life fall apart? The house, the routine, his arms around her, his kiss on the forehead, their conversations late at night about what's next, their daydreaming about owning a boat, their dog, their friends, their places? All of it was gone, like a sandcastle destroyed in a second by a rising tide.

"Senora, you're blocking the entrance, ma'am!"

"Sorry, Pablito, bad morning." Coco finally snapped out of it, looked at Pablo, and gave him her car key.

"It's what we make of it, senora."

Finally in her office, she barely could contain her tears. She can't be emotional; it's what makes women at work unsuccessful, unfortunately, she thought. This wasn't vulnerability, this was bat-shit crazy, and it was too much for anybody to see.

"OK! Good morning…" Her PA entered the office carrying a mug and some printed scripts for her to examine. "Your coffee. Here we go. So, you got a 9 a.m. with the leadership team, then a quick creative review over the pitch at 10 a.m. You told me to remind you about…" She suddenly stopped her rant and looked at Coco, who stood there silently with teary eyes.

"Hey, are you OK?" she finally asked, then shut the door to the office.

"What? Ah yes, yes, totally fine, just allergies!" Coco replied.

"OK, well, you let me know if you need anything. I'll come back after 10, and we can look at the rest of the day, OK, hon?"

"Sounds good," Coco replied.

The PA looked worried as she left Coco's office. It wasn't the genuine type of worrying, though – more like the corporate kind of worried, which implied the danger of Coco missing work and causing scheduling horrors.

"Open or closed?" she asked as she held the door, almost probing whether those were really allergies, or Coco just needed to cry her eyes out for a quick bit.

"Closed please."

Jen nodded and closed the door.

"Oh, one last thing," she quickly rushed back, "I think your phone is out of battery or something is up with it. People can't reach you. Let me know if you need any help."

Having a full day at work and a cheating partner is definitely a version of hell nobody talks about, particularly in America. You can't pour your anger on somebody else. That's viewed as unfair. You can't show you're feeling blue because you'd be too emotional for a C suite. You can't take time off because that's completely irresponsible given the workload and just how understaffed the company was. Thus, Coco just had to grin and bear it.

She opened her phone and thought she'd see 100 notifications, 20 missed calls, and a bit of desperation from Davey. In return, she got nothing. No phone calls, no extra texts, no nothing.

"Are you fucking kidding me?" she finally texted Davey out of anger as her expectations shattered. "I'm sorry," Davey replied. "Seriously, like you didn't even notice my phone was down? I could've been dead for all you care, I bet," wrote Coco, angry and acting like the crazy woman she never wanted to be. "I didn't realize your phone was off. You stopped answering my texts anyway," replied Davey. "Can we do this face to face instead of texts?" he continued. "Fine. Meet me at 1 p.m. at Casa Lavender."

Coco so desperately wanted to talk to someone about this, about how the man she spent the last two years with suddenly decided to cheat on her with Rebbekah Levy. But who could she call and for what reason? The only logical way she'd call a friend is if she had decided to leave Davey. Otherwise, how do you tell somebody your partner cheated, then you decided to stay with him? How would people look at you after that? How would people look at your relationship? In a world of open options, in which you always can be happier, staying in a relationship after cheating is the new shame, instead of not breaking it apart as it once was when her parents started dating. However, statistically, 95% of couples stay together after cheating. At least for a short while, they find a way to rekindle what they once had.

Before this very moment, Coco always said that if a man ever cheated on her, she'd leave – that this is where she drew the line. However, once you're standing in front of that line you've drawn, you start thinking what would constitute the kind of infidelity that would make you never cross that line. You see, the definition of that line, just like the definition of infidelity, changes over time because you rewrite your own code of relationship conduct.

What was the kind of cheating Coco was willing to accept? A one-night stand? Sexting? A virtual relationship? A fling? For all she knew, Rebbekah Levy could've been any of the above, so if she was to continue the relationship with Davey, she had to decide what she could move on with before she found out the real story behind those texts.

As she walked into Casa Lavender, she saw Davey standing at their table, facing the Fifth Avenue entrance to Central Park. He always cleaned up well. He was tall and gorgeous as usual. Two years into the relationship, she still didn't get used to just how good he looked, how well he dressed. He could still grab her hand, and she would feel the electricity she felt when they first dated. Perhaps there were no giant swallowtails in her belly anymore, but there were definitely still some small Buckeyes still flattering their wings every time their eyes met.

"Thank you for coming," said Davey as he grabbed her chair for her to sit down.

"I don't want to make a drama out of this; I want us to be mature about it," Coco replied. "I don't care when it started, for how long it was..."

"It was nothing. Nothing. A stupid thing," Davey insisted, "a stupid thing I didn't realize would cause so much harm."

"Did you sleep with her?" asked Coco with a clear-cut, serious voice, though realistically, she didn't really want to know the answer to that.

"What difference does it make?" asked Davey.

"Did you sleep with her?" asked Coco once again.

"Listen, this thing, it was a stupid mistake," answered Davey, but Coco quickly interrupted "You didn't?"

"No, let me finish," Davey continued. "You can behave all your life right. You could be always on time, always faithful, never doing any stupid thing. Then one day, for one moment, you slip, and that becomes your legacy. Think about all the stories about this one guy who had one glass too many and though he never, ever, ever drinks and drives, one night, he decides he was so close to home that he can drive home, instead of hailing a cab. One moment in time when he crossed that line he drew for himself. One moment. That's all it took for him to get in a car drunk, crash into another car, and leave a kid without a mother and his wife without a husband. One moment – that's all it took. That's what this was – one moment, one stupid mistake, but this can't be our legacy. We can't undo our past, but we can do so much more for our future."

Coco was listening quietly. She tried to read between the lines as Davey always knew how to answer tricky questions.

"So, you did sleep with her?"

"No, I didn't."

"Are you in love with her?" asked Coco.

"No, I'm not. I'll end this right away."

"End what?" asked Coco, though she knew exactly what he meant.

"This… Rebbekah Levy. Whatever THIS is," Davey reassured her.

"How do we move on from here, Davey? Tell me, how do I ever trust you again? How do I know this won't happen again? That two years from now, we won't be in the same exact place, when you tell me this motivational story about moving on, and I have to find the power to move past my integrity, lie to myself we're all good, and smile and wave to our friends and family. How, Davey, how?"

Davey looked at her and stood still. He realized the pain he inflicted upon Coco, but knew that nothing he could say would make it better.

"Do you need time? Do you want to stay somewhere else, or do you want me to go stay at my folks for a couple days?"

"Are you throwing me out now?"

"What? No. I just want to give you space."

Coco looked straight into his eyes, but she barely could see him anymore though because tears had flooded her eyes, and she didn't want to blink and allow him to see her cry. So, she stood up instead.

"Desires may run deep, Davey, but betrayals leave scars."

"Coco…"

"I'll stay in a hotel for a few days." She then turned her back to Davey, mad that he still called her Coco.

She left Davey behind in Casa Lavender – no fuss, no tears, no hassle. Or at least, not that he knew of anyway. Contrary to what she'd hoped for and to be fair to what any woman would expect, Davey didn't run after her, beg her to stay, swear a lifetime of cheesy lines and unconditional love, wasn't crying "I'm sorry." Davey stayed behind – not because he didn't care, but because that's just not who he was. Coco knew it, or maybe she made that excuse for him a long time ago. Truthfully, it wasn't the daily grind that made her fall in love, but mere imagination. Rational Coco would agree that there must be some sort of study to prove imagination was the culprit of the biggest disappointments in every relationship. Too bad love is irrational.

They say affairs redefine a couple, setting the future to what they become. Will they part ways, stick together and grow stronger, or will she just stick around, afraid to be single again, and he'll continue to do what probably he'd been doing for a while now? People don't change, or do they? In that moment, she kind of felt the need to believe they do, but Coco was nowhere near a position to decide what their couple legacy will be, so she made the smartest and toughest decision she could make – to stay away. She checked into the Icy Hotel the same day, pulled the curtains, and went to bed by 7 p.m.

Her body and mind were in such a state of shock that she wasn't even crying; she couldn't cry. Instead of counting sheep, her mind kept going round and round and round on every single detail of their relationship. Every word, phrase, text, kiss, gesture, every time he worked late, and every time he didn't answer his phone. Four hours later, she decided there's no point in trying to go to sleep and resorted to a sleeping pill she remembered she saved from the time she had a work pitch, and anxiety didn't let her rest. She finally chose personal life to work. Isn't that ironic?

A few hours later, disturbed by the sunrise reflecting rays off the high-rise across the street and through the window she forgot to pull the curtains on, Coco woke up. The room felt cold, though it was summer, and the AC could barely keep up with the heat. But that's the thing with hotels – no matter how much they cost, no matter how they look, no matter how fine their linen is, they'll always feel cold, as they'll never be home. And when your home is wrecked, they're even farther away from what the feeling of a home should be. Now, having the strength to stay in that horrible state of mind is no easy task. There also must be a study somewhere out there that showed people getting back together because they miss the familiarity of their home, and she would agree. It's one thing to walk out the door; it's a totally different thing to leave your home.

To Coco's credit, she managed to stay there for a week, curtains pulled for several days, ordering in and ignoring her phone. Not an easy task for a woman of her professional stature, but luckily she wasn't saving lives. She was creating ads, and every now and then, advertising could wait for an imaginary stomach bug she made up to be able to avoid work. In bed for days, she wanted to text Davey, but she carefully wrote potential texts as notes first, not directly in the chat, because god forbid she might send it by mistake. The problem is, she never sent them. And slowly, she built a journal of pain in her notes, a journal locked forever in her cloud, as she was meticulous about syncing.

When she returned home from the hotel a few days later, the house was quiet – even more quiet than she remembered it, she thought. However, the moment she walked in, she felt instantly comfortable. There's something so truthfully cliche about *home sweet home* – the feeling that waking up in the same space, with the same routine, can give you. As an introvert, Coco was entrapped by her own routines and habits, so it was easy to fall back into that web and cave in to what once was. Davey wasn't home, no flowers were waiting for her – no Sarah Jessica Parker moment. But it was quiet and comfortable, and after six nights at the dreadful Icy Hotel in Midtown, all she wanted was the quiet of the fourth floor in Dumbo, overseeing Manhattan and the Brooklyn Bridge.

It all flashed back before eyes, when she and Davey saw the place for the first time – the large windows she fell in love with, the awkwardly spacious rooms for an apartment in New York City, and the view. She remembered Davey, who had a typical Wall Street guy obsession with expensive watches, pointing to the Dumbo clock tower and recognizing it:

"That's definitely in the top 20 most expensive watches in the world," he pointed out as he held Coco's waist.

"That?" Asked Coco in disbelief.

"Yup. That loft in the tower that holds it was just bought for $4.25 million by Anne Hathaway."

Coco now stood in that same spot, imagining his arms around her waist, then smiled. Can Rebbekah Levy truly shatter their years of history and the ones their future had in store? Entire books can be written about the conversations with Davey that followed –

conversations anyone who ever has been cheated on is very familiar with: He took responsibility for his actions, spent more time at home, and paid more attention to what she wanted and what made sense for them as a family. However, out of all the conversations that followed, a seed was planted in Coco's head: To this day, she's not sure whether it was her therapist or her married and depressed friend who advised her to remain in the relationship, but this seed was the seed of the idea that it was their sex life that drove him to infidelity. Was it her? Coco never would admit to this in front of any friend and perhaps not even her therapist, but their sex life up to that point wasn't great for unknown reasons. It made absolutely no sense. They had so much chemistry together, and yet that love bubble didn't burst in bed. The problem was that while most things can be solved through conversations in a relationship, sex wasn't really one of them for Coco and Davey. The more they talked about it, the more it worked against them because it made them cerebral in bed, thinking about the actions they had to make to satisfy one another, making any sense of spontaneity disappear. It was like karma was coming back to bite her. She remembered the time she cheated on an ex because of sex. She was reading a book at the time and fell into the trap of wanting a fictional relationship that was impossible to get in real life. What if Davey was now experiencing the same? What if he watched so much porn that his expectations in bed were unmet in life by the missionary position?

Coco soon became someone else. Sexually. Hours and hours of therapy told her that it might have been her at fault all along and that she needed to reignite her passion for erotism, for femininity. It was as if someone had placed a mirror in front of her and made her question her own femininity – how she walked, dressed before sex, touched her husband, brushed her hair, and behaved in bed. All of it was now staring back at her, in the mirror, questioning whether she was as good in her sexual life as she was in her day-to-day life. She always thought she was a bit promiscuous, that she was sexual enough. But what was in her head never actually ever materialized in bed. She wanted to have a threesome with another woman, but never had the courage to go all the way. She wanted to wear string lingerie or try role play, but never did. When she was an adolescent, she used to masturbate imagining her husband came back late and had sex with her, really hard. When she was 14, she used to masturbate thinking a very rich prince would fall for her and want her badly. However, in her 30s, it was all pretty missionary. The reality was that in her head, Coco always had been adventurous, but in reality, she always had been quite a prude. For reasons she couldn't really understand, she had suppressed that sexuality, and only she could bring it back to life. She started sending nudes to Davey and demanded wild sex from him, which, contrary to what she had expected from a man, triggered a self-defense mechanism from her husband. Why did she want this? Why now? Why like this? Slowly,

Davey caved in, and they became a little closer – both in bed and in real life. For a second there, all seemed better. Davey was back into her, Rebbekah Levy was a thing of the past, and Coco was, for once, the center of his love. Until September 4.

On September 4, Coco arrived home late from work. It was quite weird for a Friday evening, but advertising life is so unpredictable that even Davey, a Wall Street guy, got used to it. When Coco got home that night, she found Davey prepping dinner and setting up drinks for her and his work colleague, Lindsey. Coco had heard about Lindsey before – a little bit from the media, a little bit from Davey. She was the most feared woman on Wall Street, devourer of men and whisperer of blue chips. She could smell a stock dip in a second, and the stocks to short in minutes. Lindsey was Coco, but a high-finance version of her, and surely more sexual than her. Coco had a fascination about her – her long hair, long bangs covering her green eyes, her sexy freckles all over her body, her big breasts and long legs. She looked like an erotica cover, only it was the cover of *Forbes* magazine. However, on September 4, Lindsey was in her kitchen, and Coco had no idea what she was doing there.

"Honey, you're home!" said Davey and gave Coco an awkwardly big hug. "Come, sit, meet Lindsey!"

Coco reached out her hand to greet Lindsey, but Lindsey leaned in and gave her a big hug, pressing her big breasts upon Coco's flat chest.

"I'm so happy to finally meet you," she said. "I've heard so much about you; Davey just won't stop talking about you. He's really proud of you. I literally know every project, every pitch, and every award you've won, girl!" said Lindsey while grabbing Coco's waist real tight.

Coco blushed. This powerful woman in her living room – Lindsey Strauss – knew all about her. But Lindsey also was sending weird signals. Was this a friends-catching-up dinner, or was it something else? Well, they were never friends. Was this business? Lindsey was two tequila shots too far in to talk about ETFs and the real value of Bitcoin. Was Davey cheating? He's not that dumb to be caught in the act. So, what was this?

"It's just three tired friends loosening up after a hard week at work!" said Davey. And Coco bought it.

Coco took off her suit and changed into something more comfortable – a silky loungewear dress – before sitting down near Lindsey, still a little threatened by her presence in her own house and not sure what the deal was between Davey and her. As she sat down, Lindsey looked at her with her big green eyes and smiled, placed her left hand on Coco's right leg and saluted.

"There you are. I love your dress!"

"Thank you!" said Coco, "I'm starving!." Lindsey removed her hand from Coco's leg and picked up the fork hitting the table with it "Chef! Hurry up! We're starving, and we don't have all night!"

Davey executed the chief's orders and delivered the best stir fry they've had all week. It was delicious – like, Michelin star delicious – the kind of dish you don't mess around with because it was cooked to perfection. However, Lindsey seemed like she never wanted to follow any rules, so the moment Davey got up to go to the restroom, Lindsey decided to go wild.

"Here, you have to try it like this!" said Lindsey, dipping her fork with noodles into a small bowl of Sriracha sauce. "I know it seems very pedestrian, but trust me, just trust me," she insisted, pushing her fork toward Coco's mouth. Though a bit hesitant, not being a huge fan of spicy food, Coco caved in and tasted it – suddenly, her whole body burst into flames, and a heatwave took over her groins all the way to her forehead and made her scream, "Ah! Hot, hot, hot! Too hot."

Lindsey started to laugh and handed Coco a glass of water while again putting her left hand on her right leg, only this time, a little bit closer to her pelvic area: "Haha. No, you're hot!" Lindsey locked her eyes onto Coco's and said nothing else, but Coco realized right there and then why Lindsey was there, why Davey brought her there after her sexual awakening, so she went for it – she grabbed Lindsey's curly hair and kissed her. The more she kissed her soft lips, the more she wanted her. The more she felt her large breasts, the more she wanted her naked. The more she unbuttoned her shirt, the more she wanted to go all in. And although Coco was scared, Lindsey was all

142

in, as she had done this before. She opened her shirt in the blink of an eye and dragged Coco's lips onto her nipples. Coco's tongue went full circles onto both of them until Lindsey slowly disappeared all the way down between Coco's legs. She started to touch her black panties with her fingers and slowly drifted them away, so she can go full-circle on Coco too. Again, and again, and again, and again. It didn't matter that Davey was there, looking at them and touching himself on the couch. Coco was in heaven, and Lindsey was waiting for her turn. Again, and again, and again – and aaaagain. When it was all over, and Coco looked around and saw Davey, she stopped and wondered whom she had become – whom they had become. Are they this twisted swinger family now? Was she into girls? No, not really, no more so than any average woman who's been curious about what doing it with a girl would be like at some time in their lives. Was she into multiple partners at once? Not really, except these past few months when her quest to find her inner femininity, turns out, went sideways. She got up, washed her face and mouth, and went to sleep – no goodbyes, no questions asked, nothing. Pure silence and confusion. Was anything else going to happen between Lindsey and Davey after she went to sleep? At this point, she didn't care anymore. The rules of the game already had changed, and there's no way that she'll win at it, so she went for the finish line as any dignified relationship athlete would do, hoping that next time, she'll be the one setting the rules, and she'll be the only one who can win.

When she got up the next morning, Davey was sleeping next to her with his arms wrapped around her waist. She didn't feel this morning embrace for a very long time. The warmth of his body, the strength of his arms surrounding her as she watched the most expensive *watch* in the world through her window – all of it took her back to the moment they fell in love again. Like *Groundhog Day*, each time they had a fight, that clock was giving Coco reasons to try again.

She got up slowly from bed, slightly afraid of what she would find in the living room. Was Lindsey gone? Will she see things she never asked for? As she climbed down the stairs to the living room, she found peace. It was sunny, the place was clean as if a SWAT cleaning team came in after she went to bed, Lindsey was gone, and everything seemed to have been just an erotic dream. However, Lindsey's forgotten earring on the floor reminded her that though it was gone, it was all real.

As she made her morning coffee, Coco again started to question her marriage to Davey. Was this it? Was this how she was supposed to live her life? Had she become this wife who was so afraid of losing her husband that she would just do anything to satisfy his needs? It made absolutely no sense. She was financially independent, in her mid-30s, was still young enough to find someone else and start another family, was famous in her field of work, was in the upper quadrants of beauty, and yet she was numb – numb to take a stand in front of him, voice her fears, and walk away. After all, last night had nothing to do with Davey: It was her choice to fool around with Lindsey, and yet, was it really her choice?

As she sipped her coffee and looked at the most expensive *watch* in the world, she remembered her mom's struggle while she was in high school. She had seen her mom crying many times that she wasn't happy in her relationship. She was so miserable that she barely could hide it from her own kids anymore. At 17 years old, Coco begged her mom to leave her dad – not because he was aggressive or a cheating bastard, but because he made her mom unhappy. Her mom wanted to remain in that relationship so that the family didn't shatter. Coco grew up like that, and she always swore she'd be independent. She grew up fantasizing about running away, yet never did anything about it. Running away from home. Running away from her hometown. Running away from her country. Running away from her relationship. That was her imaginary coping mechanism. A sort of *Catch Me if You Can* in real life, a Julia Roberts in *Runaway Bride* sort of thing. The only difference was she always stayed put, as she was running away only in her imagination. Sometimes at night, she dreamed that Davey left her, then wake up crying, thankful they were still together. Loneliness was too scary for her.

By Instagram standards, they were perfect for each other. They were right up there with #couplegoals or #powercouple. He was her Mr. Big, and she was his Carrie Bradshaw, always caressing and hugging in public. They seemed like they couldn't get enough of each other, but Coco was in advertising and knew exactly how to build her own personal brand and create a unique selling proposition, even if it was a house of cards. Suddenly, her moment of inner dialogue, a bit different from what a "me moment" looks like in a coffee commercial, was interrupted by Davey.

"Morning babe. Sleep well?"

"Are you kidding me!?" thought Coco, but replied casually, "Yeah, pretty good. You?"

Davey nodded his head *"yes"* as he yawned and poured himself a big cup of coffee. Coco was screaming inside, as she did so many times before, but didn't let it out and contained herself like the atypical Virgo that she was.

"You still up for tonight at Patrick's?" screamed Davey while brushing his teeth, barely speaking the words right as his mouth was full of toothpaste. Shit. Coco had forgotten about Patrick's party, which was quite frustrating for her, as she had dreamed about that party all week. "Yeah, still on," she screamed back at Davey, slightly afraid of it, but desperately trying to keep up with this new person she seems like she had become – work hard, play hard, right? Well – she was about to find out.

As Davey exited the bathroom, Coco knew that look on his face and had seen it before. It was the look of "I don't want to talk about it." She sighed in relief as she most definitely didn't want to talk about what happened the previous night with Lindsey either. The real question was – will Lindsey be at Patrick's party tonight? THAT would be weird by all standards. One can only hope she won't be.

***

Patrick was, you guessed it, another Wall Street guy. He was perhaps the very definition of a Wall Street guy – a good mix between a crook and an accountant, a protein-pumped bodybuilder and an overworked corporate executive who was rich. Very rich. Ridiculously rich. After all, he was the main partner in Patrick & Stanley investment group. People say his company focused a lot on investments in underdeveloped countries, mainly in Africa, because they believed the next big thing was there. However, those closer to the matter knew there was an off-grid affiliation between Patrick & Stanley and four blockchain companies that were driving the financial revolution forward. Of course, Coco understood almost none of this. Although married to a finance guy, she never really understood how investments or the stock market worked, nor did she really care. To her, it was all a Ponzi scheme designed for people with doctorates in economics.

He lived in the new Jenga Tower in Manhattan that he helped finance – in the penthouse, comprising two floors and 12 rooms, plus an outdoor swimming pool in the clouds. An article in *Architecture Today* claimed it was among the top 50 most expensive homes in New York City, valued at $85 million. So, as you can imagine, every New Yorker who mattered was at that party, with phone battery fully charged and ready to connect at full-speed Internet strength for Instagram stories, tags, power play posts for LinkedIn, and anything in between. It was like the Met Gala, but for Wall Street folks, so nobody was about to miss it.

As Coco and Davey walked into the Jenga Tower penthouse, the party met their expectations. Every heir self-proclaimed as a socialite on their curated Wikipedia page, every investor featured in *Forbes*, every analyst who did at least one interview on Bloomberg, every woman on Raya, and every self-made millionaire were there. The party lied at the intersection of a public affairs event and a friend's party, leaning more toward the former.

"David fucking Robinson! I can't believe it – the man himself. How the hell are you, bro?" screamed Patrick from the other side of the room as Coco and Davey walked in.

"Can't miss Sir Patrick's emancipation party," replied David in the same bro manner as he was greeted.

"Hahaha. Fuck you, man! Coco, I hope I can call you Coco by now," asked Patrick, while Coco, the intuitive communication person that she was, nodded.

"Sure," though she thought that was way too patronizing for a man of his stature.

"You look stunning as always," he continued, sort of patching his way into her liking, though Coco was sure he barely could remember what she looked like in the first place because the last time they met in St. Barth's on their vacation, Patrick was super high on coke, and they barely were into their first cocktail of the evening.

"Thank you for having us, Patrick. We've been looking forward to seeing what the big fuss is about with this new penthouse in Manhattan," Coco punched back.

"Haha. Feisty! Well, trust me Coco, this is it. The house that will have more pictures taken than Versailles and more women laid than the Playboy Mansion itself. Much better than Madison Avenue, am I right? Hahaha." Patrick then fist-bumped David.

Coco smiled, but cringed on the inside, rolling the eyes of her soul and questioning how such an asshole can have so much money and be so successful at what he does. He was talented, no doubt, so she naturally blamed his social behavior on what most woman would – his small dick.

Patrick quickly passed Coco and Davey to his assistant, who, as one could imagine, was looking like a *Shark Tale* character, with oversized lips and breasts, but who was fluent in five languages and was really kind to them. So, Coco decided that she was being too judgmental about her certainly much-paid-for body additions and wanted to be nice to her. After all, the assistant lived and worked close to that asshole every day.

The penthouse was out of this world. It had 16-foot-high ceilings across the entire house, with bathrooms covered in Lux Touch Marble, which ran about $100,000 for 10 square feet. Coco wasn't good at math, but she easily could tell that this was a lot of money. It came with nine bedrooms with en suite baths, divided by a glass wall that could change its brightness with the push of a button. The master bedroom was as big as Coco's apartment, with a 430-square-foot color-coded dressing room, a 300-square-foot bathroom, and a private terrace with a private pool that had a glass bottom. On the same top floor was an entertainment room containing a cinema, some vintage video games, and a poker table. That night, the poker table had a professional poker dealer waiting to entertain guests, but instead of dealing cards, she was dealing cocaine. All you had to do for one line of New York's finest was to play a hand of blackjack with her.

"Does it matter if we win or not?" asked Davey.

"The only thing that matters is to play the game," replied the poker dealer with a French accent, transporting the guest into the ambiance of a high-end Monte Carlo casino.

Davey turned around to Coco and asked her. "Wanna play?" Coco hesitated, feeling like she already acted weird enough that weekend, so she suggested:

"Perhaps later. Let's at least finish the tour." Davey approved of her suggestion and promised the cocaine blackjack dealer that they'd return.

Patrick's assistant smiled and called for a bartender to serve them two glasses of Ruinart Blanc de Blancs, which coincidentally was Coco's favorite champagne, as their tour of the house ended. Coco took a sip of the drink, and as she placed her glass on the marble bar in front of them, she noticed a red-haired woman on the other side of the room. It was Lindsey, who lifted up her glass to salute her from afar in a very polite and diplomatic way. Coco did the same, thinking, "Please don't come here, please don't come here." But Lindsey was too cocky, too Wall Street not to come there.

"Hello, my darling. How are you?" Lindsey asked Coco while kissing her on both cheeks. Coco stiffened. It was too sudden for her to even begin to understand whether she was turned on by Lindsey or whether she felt that her intimacy was trespassed.

"Good, good. We just got here and did the tour of the house," replied Coco, unwittingly. "It's gorgeous, isn't it? So airy, so spacey. I'd say it's very, very Patrick." Coco kept looking for Lindsey to give her verbal hints that she's hitting on her, but she got nothing – Lindsey was corporate-friendly.

Suddenly, a tall brunette with long straight hair approached them. She had legs that would keep going underneath her beautiful shiny drape-like dress, with green eyes and a lovely British accent.

"Hey, this is Annabelle. She works at Pattrick & Stanley and is a financial analyst. Annabelle, this is Coco." Coco was furious.

Why did all these Wall Street assholes feel like they can demean who she was, what her career was? After all, she's one of the top five most influential women of the year according to *FW* magazine, so who the hell was Lindsey to demean her? Coco quickly grabbed another glass of Ruinart and chugged it.

"OK, we gotta go mingle a bit. Nice to see you again, Coco. Before you leave, make sure you deal a poker hand at the dealer's table. Loosen up – it's Manhattan," Lindsey said, as she disappeared into the crowd with Annabelle. Coco could swear she saw Lindsey grabbing Annabelle's ass as they vanished, but yet again, it also could've been just her sick imagination.

Davey was now gone from her line of sight. Coco looked around for him, but couldn't find him. Her second glass was already empty, and she thought she needed a third to survive the night, so she picked up another and went up the stairs to see whether she could find Davey there. After all, she didn't know anybody else at the party but Patrick the asshole, Lindsey, and now Annabelle, and she was in no state of mind to network.

Coco found Davey upstairs in the entertainment room with three other Wall Street douchebags. It seemed like they started a real game of Texas Hold'em. The winner would have to snort a line from the decks of cards, which by popular belief was a win-win situation. Davey was on a winning streak.

"Coco! Come, sit down, play a round," Davey enthusiastically screamed at Coco. "Hey, everybody, this is my one-of-a-kind wife." He then outstretched his arms and gave her a big kiss on her lips.

"Coco," she introduced herself, giving in to what everyone on Wall Street now called her anyway.

The dealer handed her two cards: a queen of hearts and a king of spades. Of course, she had high cards and had no intention of snorting cocaine tonight, yet the universe just decided it was going to be a long night for her. She had to be a player and play the part, but not all hope was lost. Three more cards to go.

Coco called, and so did everybody else. Next, she got a jack of spades. Coco still had nothing, but it could be she's headed for a straight. Steve, one of the players, placed a bet – one line of coke. Davey called, and so did Jeffrey. Coco followed. Second card dealt: a 10 of hearts. Coco thought, "Are you kidding me???" But she called, and thought there was enough. Unfortunately for her, everybody called. Last dealt card – an ace. Coco clearly just won, but she called, bluffing, hoping the game would go on. Yet everyone called once again. Cards on the table – her future tonight was there, lying on the table, as weird cocaine tarot cards. She braved herself, rolled a dollar bill and snorted it. The rush combined with a burning sensation immediately kicked in. Davey kissed her on the forehead almost as if he tried to calm her down, helping her get up from the table – it was enough coke poker for one night.

After a few more hours of mingling at New York's most exclusive party, Davey wanted a break, so he quickly snagged Coco and went upstairs to hide in Patrick's bedroom. Was it because it was still empty, and he knew it wouldn't be for long, or was it because he genuinely wanted some time off? Coco didn't care much. They were married, somewhat happy, had the world on a plate, and nothing mattered. The coke took over her thinking, and she was dynamite – super-extroverted, open, and happy to chat about what truly brought her joy. As they walked into the bedroom, Coco never felt more in love. Cocaine does that to you. It amplifies the smallest feeling you have and blows it out of proportion. However, with Coco, it could've gone sideways and amplified the feeling of remorse she had for many things that went on in her relationship, but the universe had something else in store for her and Davey that night – love.

They went out on the private terrace and stared at the lightly polluted sky, hoping to catch a glimpse of a star over New York City. All they got in return was an American Airlines jet landing at La Guardia in the middle of the night, looking like a modern falling star.

"What's next for us?" Coco suddenly asked.

Davey looked at her and grabbed her hand.

"What do you mean? We're good, aren't we?"

"Yes," replied Coco, "but how long are we going to keep going like this?"

"Like what?" Davey was intrigued, and Coco now had his full attention.

"THIS. Out by night, in the office by day. I'm tired. Drinking, blowing, working too much, burning too much, not growing up. I – I'm tired."

"Coco, look around you. Look where you are. Other people would kill to be here in this place right now. Look who's around you – you have the finest people in New York hugging and fist-bumping you."

"God, I hope they're not fist-bumping me," Coco laughed.

"Do you think Paula from Silver Heights High School would ever dream of this? She has three kids and barely has time to breathe, that poor woman. Is that what you want?" Paula was Coco's best friend in high school. She remained in their hometown, became a doctor, and had three wonderful kids. Coco talked to her all the time. It was one of those friendships that, although they've taken very different paths in life, their relationship never faded. However, Davey never really cared for Paula and thought she was too pedestrian for him.

"Maybe. Maybe it's time to grow up. I don't want to die alone," she continued.

Davey turned around.

"Seriously, Davey, I want to have a family. I want to build the family I'm missing right now. I mean, we're doing well in our careers, we earn enough money, and we can put a kid through college. We should just have a kid."

"Just have a kid? Why? Do you want a kid, or do you just feel like that's something we need to tick off our list?"

Silence settled in for a moment, and they only could hear the chatter and laughter from downstairs. For some people, the most important conversations somehow always happen in the most unsuitable moments. Downstairs, people were talking business, travel, living the life. Upstairs, right there on their balcony, the future was unfolding, and a change of life was being discussed. Under the influence. Unfortunately, there's no law against having life-changing conversations when you're under the influence. The only court of law in this case is how your life unravels further. If you aren't a very good lawyer of your own life, you could go to your own jail for life – a place where you're so constrained, and your life is so shattered that there are very few options for you to get out.

"Do you think we'd be good parents though?" Davey broke the silence "I don't think I'm ready, Coco."

"You'd be a great father. I know it!" Coco enthusiastically replied without really substantiating her positivity.

"I don't want to end up like my dad. I'm too hedonistic. I don't think it's the best decision we can make. Do you want all THIS to stop?"

"Why should it stop?"

"Because a kid changes you forever, Coco. It's no longer about you; it's about the baby."

"But then what's next for us? Are we going to do this forever?"

"We're always traveling. How would we take care of the baby?"

"Nannies"

"But how many nannies? You can barely stand anybody else but us in the house. How would you stand a nanny?"

"It's just the normal thing to do next, Davey."

"We'll see." Davey then kissed Coco on the forehead and got up.

Coco got up and followed him, barely walking straight at this point, all boozed up by way of too many glasses. As she stepped into Patrick's bedroom, she saw Davey sitting on the bed.

"Can you believe this place?"

"It's insane," Coco replied and sat down beside him.

"You think we'll ever get a place like this?"

"We can only hope so." Coco lied down. "I told you I'll be filthy rich one day." Then she laughed.

"This is filthy." Davey then looked around and smiled. He lied down next to Coco and grabbed her hand.

Coco grabbed his hand and kissed it. He turned around and looked at her, their eyes locked. He kissed her and started to unbutton her shirt. *"Let's have a baby,"* Davey said, then smiled.

***

When she found out she was pregnant, she wasn't surprised. She somehow knew and felt it before her period was late, before she got nausea, before two lines appeared on her pregnancy test. As a woman, most of the time, you know.

But there's something about unplanned pregnancies that she felt wasn't spoken about enough – how they shake your very identity and make you question whom you want to become next, whom you want to live your life with, and how you want to live it. Society has been mostly a fan of just one side of the coin – the side where motherhood is being praised and applauded as a way to make a woman feel complete. If you're 35 and without kids, your biological clock is ticking. If you're married without children, something must be wrong. You're selfish, you're shallow, and/or you don't understand the meaning of life. You should be thankful for those who have children because they'll be the ones paying back society when you're old, etc.

When she found out she was pregnant, Coco felt all that pressure and asked herself all these questions. She wasn't ready to be a mom. It was the biological clock, the marriage, the societal pressure that made her confused, and in a moment of weakness, her blurred mind decided she should have a baby. Then when the "baby" happened, the universe placed a big mirror in front of her and said, "Now let's see if you're ready."

However, Coco wasn't ready, even though society told her differently, partly because she was superficial, partly because of all the drama in her life, but mostly because she wasn't ready to give up her independence. She grew up in a house with a mom who was dependent on her dad, and it's that dependency that infiltrated Coco's childhood, through unhappiness and her mom's death. Coco swore she'd never become dependent, that as long as she's healthy, she'll be responsible for her well-being, and that nothing will stop her from doing this. And yet, inside her womb, there's now a baby, a 4-week-old embryo growing inside. When she went to the doctor, the judging eyes, the nodding of the head, and the questioning of "Are you sure you want to have an abortion?" consumed her from within and made her question her very identity. Was she mom material? Was she about to do all the baby work, be responsible for another human being for the rest of her life, and find joy in it? Was she ready to be "complete"? Was something wrong with her?

Like everyone else, she read all the stories about the working mom, about the founder of Bumble who is now a billionaire and rang the bell at NSYU with a baby in her arms, proving that you can do it all. She read about women being a force of nature, and how all these women felt transformed and found new meaning in life after giving birth, but she also felt that a lot of it was pressure, a social media hoax, a picture that hides a thousand words. Friends were having babies all around her. Everywhere she turned, someone was expecting, giving birth, or trying to conceive. So, what the hell was wrong with her? Why was she still dubious?

Was it because Davey reacted so bad to it? Was it her who didn't feel ready, or was it him? It made no sense for her not to be ready. As she felt funny noises in her tummy, she looked in the mirror, and for a second, she felt warmth. She knew there was something there that she could love forever – something special, something hard to explain. She felt that if she let it go, some would say it's murder. She was 35, and there's a human being inside of her, and if she had an abortion, terminated that baby, stopped that soul from growing, she would stop the possibility of a new life.

Somehow, people believe that women who get abortions by choice and for no other reason have no remorse, no second thoughts, and don't feel anything. They're robots. Well, to Coco, that was the most dehumanizing thing in the abortion process. She felt so conflicted that she couldn't discuss it with anybody else. The night she told David she was pregnant, it was nothing like you'd see on a pregnancy-reveal video on social media or in a video mix during the *Ellen* TV talk show. It was nothing like *Sex and the City*, when Mr.

Big comes around and settles down to marry Carrie. It was nothing like that. It was the opposite. David had a mix of anxiety, anger, guilt and everything in between in a burst that lasted perhaps one minute. Just one. He then turned around and left for a meeting. Coco wasn't expecting him to be thrilled, but she also never expected him to react like that. It felt like he made the whole experience about him, his desires, his fears, and nothing about her, as if she tricked him into it, as if she had a different agenda that she was hiding from him. Thus, Coco did what any woman would: she left.

Not for good, but just for now, to allow for silence to settle in so that she could actually hear her inner thoughts. Just hers and no one else's. Unfortunately, "no one else's thoughts" is a very abstract concept unless you're living off the grid in the middle of nowhere. Today, everybody has an opinion – the friend you've confided in, your therapist, your newspaper, that article you read the other day. Directly and indirectly, even if they don't know you, everybody has a say in it, and you can't shut everybody down.

Everywhere she looked now, she saw babies. Shuffling on insta-stories? Babies. On her girls' messaging group? Another picture of a baby or another pregnancy announced. When she decided to quit social media and just watch some Netflix to clear her head, the streamer's suggestions always included some random family movie with kids or some teen pregnancy show. In stores, beyond her control, she always picked the entrance through the kids' section, as if the universe was showing her the middle finger for fighting against what was set to occur naturally.

After a while, solitude settled in, then a sense of confusion, loneliness, and lack of meaning creeped in. As a woman, there's a part of you that makes you feel like a failure no matter what your brain says. Coco was faced once again with another imposture of playing nice, of acting against her values of truth, but this time, she wondered whether she actually could live by her values and admit what she truly wanted. This wasn't a decision she could sweep under the rug or lie about. If this was to work out, for her sanity, she needed to be open and direct about it, and committed to it.

A baby changes your life, whether you keep it or not. If you keep the baby, it makes your life happier and more fulfilled – at least according to society. If you don't, it makes you question your womanhood and where your life is headed. Either way, it changes it – permanently.

She instinctively knew where she stood: she wasn't ready to be a mother. No matter what the world would think of her, no matter how much she'd be judged for it. So, without asking for permission, without putting it up for debate, she decided not to think about it anymore and take charge of her own body and destiny.

***

The noise from a small refrigerator next to the other bed was the only thing she could hear. It was possibly the first white noise that wasn't soothing to her, causing more anxiety than she wanted. She stared at the painting in front of her in the maternity ward that portrayed a woman nursing her newborn baby and felt nothing. The doctor was mumbling something. She could acknowledge it, but she was numb.

"We have to talk about contraceptives when this is over" said the doctor, but it was more like a faint ringing in her ear. She felt ridiculous to have that conversation at her age.

As she looked at the hormone-blocking pills the doctor gave her, she felt a sense of relief, unlike everything else she felt up until that day. The attention was back on her – about the symptoms she felt, not about what the world would think about it. Was it wrong that she had no had feelings against Davey? Was she wrong that she didn't hold him accountable? Was she wrong about everything?

The bed in front of her was empty, and it felt like a bad lottery: surely the next woman to occupy that bed will be a woman giving birth – yet another slap in the face.

Friends support you through thick and thin, but the reality is that a baby changes them too. Coco shared what she was going through with very few friends – only the close ones. However, even they judged her silently. The entire world turned around her and had an opinion about her body. Perhaps many thought she wouldn't go through with it "What's wrong with you? You're married, doing well – so keep the baby. He/she was sent by the universe." Coco let these thoughts play with her for a while. This was one of those moments when she needed somebody with her more than anything, but she didn't have anyone to turn to.

For a second, Coco stopped and wondered why there's nothing abnormal about a man not having children, but it's completely wrong for women not to have any. Furthermore, she never said she wouldn't have children, but rather that this wasn't the time for it. She took the first pill, and suddenly a burst of pain hit her belly like a fist in the gut. The process had started. Another punch, then another, and then another – until she was curled up, ironically, in the fetal position herself. A few hours later, it was over.

Coco waited for a feeling of regret, but she didn't feel any. She felt as if her life was given back to her, and it was now time to plan things properly. When she got out, Davey was waiting in the car, scared and pale and for the first time ever, without any clever line to make everything feel just a bit better.

***

When the alarm rang, Coco awakened scared and sweaty, with a headache the size of a hangover. It was already almost a month since she had the abortion, and now weird dreams started to creep in. The weird paradox of the Big Three G's – guilt, gumption, and grief – took over.

But this, again, was right for her and was what she wanted. Hours of therapy had proven useless again and again, until her therapist casually dropped into a conversation something that stuck with her: "You can't deny who you are." That was true. She never had been defined by family, but rather by her individual self. She had been a person who needed that freedom. Maybe this was a sign that it's not society that should tell you how to live, it's not the man whom everybody thinks you should date that makes you happy, and it's not the people who judge you for what you do that push you forward – it's you. While this probably was the most selfish thing she's ever done, while it gave her moments of confusion and grief, this was right. It was right for her, and nothing else mattered.

She turned around and looked at Davey, rolled over on the other side of the bed, holding on to a pillow in his arms like a baby. He was sleeping peacefully, detached from the reality she was now living in. One big bed was now the bridge between the two worlds that collided: hers and his. She pressed the button near the bed, and the curtains around them started to drag. The mechanism sound always relaxed her; it was the sound of a new day starting. The rays of New York beaming over "the most expensive watch in the world" were giving her hope again.

"Rise and shine. Big day ahead," mumbled Davey, still half asleep, as he turned over to her and smiled. "Yeah, big day." replied Coco, not feeling the happiness others would have probably felt in her position. Or would they? Was this the value of a life that never happened? Should she celebrate this accomplishment, or should she feel bad about the decision she made? She shook her head and turned over, placed her tiny feet into furry slippers on the soft carpet, and got out of bed.

Looking in the mirror today felt different. It was still her, but a part of her was missing. Wrinkles that weren't there before started to show, dark circles under her eyes slowly were creeping in, and she felt exhausted. She hardly could remember the last time she slept well in the past couple of months, but she always had been a person who owned up to her decisions, and she won't let this take her down. "It's just a phase..." she repeated in her head. "It's just a phase. Like many others before, like many others to come. It's just a phase."

In the mirror's reflection, she noticed her beautiful dark suit waiting for her. She had placed it the night before in the dressing room, next to her dark Dior shoes. She stared at it for a minute, almost as if questioning everything. She washed her face again and smiled. She WAS excited about this interview, WAS looking forward to this moment all her life, WAS looking to know what's next in her career and life, but WAS unavailable emotionally at this time for anybody else in her life. That's just who SHE WAS. "Don't deny who you are" she taught to herself as she stepped into her dressing room. A big pile of *FW* magazines was on the small table in the dressing room, a testament to whom she had become – a testament to hard work that paid off, of priorities being established right.

As she closed the last button of her suit; put on her Dior heels; kissed Davey, who was making coffee; said hi to her doorman as she exited the building; and got into the car waiting for her to take her to FW magazine for the Next Five interview, all of it made sense. She won't deny who she was. Not anymore.

Chapter 4

Nicole

Dear Mom,

I've always felt like my life started at that very moment. You were looking deep into my eyes, controlling tears from rushing out of your crystal-clear eyes and messing up your angelic face. You stood still and said nothing. I was crying. "I'm sorry, mom!" I said, as blood was pouring down my body out of every possible limb I had injured. I didn't feel any pain. I felt regret – regret that what I did, not what happened to me, made you cry. Little did I know that I'd see that quite often, though you gracefully tried to hide it every single time for the next 20 years. That's when it all started.

My life started on June 14, 1998 – though my actual birth was eight years earlier.

Now when I look back in time, shredding my logic into pieces and breaking down all rationale, I've come to the conclusion that life is, indeed, a cycle – a different one we all witness and are a part of. It may never look the same or feel the same, but if you open your heart widely, you'll see it coming. The end always will circle back to the beginning.

And mom, it did. We never knew how it would end, but we knew the end was coming.

And then, 20 years later, it was you who was lying on the hospital bed, taking your last breaths without even knowing it. As you laid unconsciously with your face strained from pain, I wouldn't be as strong as you were. I couldn't bear to see you in that much pain. You didn't deserve so much suffering. You didn't deserve so many tubes, needles, and patches hurting every centimeter of your tiny body. You may have looked like a different person, but your love, face, and energy still were untouched. Still, you and I couldn't stop crying. My tears rushed over my wrecked face, out of my blurry eyes, and I looked nothing like you did 20 years earlier. I wasn't the superhero you'd been all your life. Besides that death bed, I was the only mortal. A few hours later, you got your cape and flew away.

I miss you, my superhero. I always will.

Your daughter,

Nicole.

Nicole sealed the letter in an envelope, not that it mattered or that anyone would ever read it anyway, but as a gesture of closure. As a final act, she reached in her pocket, pulled a match from a Kateguhan Hotel matchbook, set the letter on fire, then threw it in the air and watched it fade away. Ashes of words and final memories flew above the Indian Ocean, carried by the Balinese wind's warmth into the dark and troubled endlessness. Nicole gazed at the sky and closed her eyes for a minute, imagining her mom was there with her on that beach, breathing in the salt of the Indian Ocean, which she always wanted to see. Nicole was tough, but there's no strength in the world, no force known to humankind that could actually stop tears when they already headed toward your cheeks. She wiped her tears, looked at the sky one last time, smiled, then headed back to the Kateguhan Hotel lobby. Chloe was waiting for her, and it was already late.

"You OK, babe?" Chloe said as she hugged Nicole.

"Yeah, let's go. We're going to miss our flight."

Truth is, Nicole got the life's-not-fair memo a year before when her mom died after a liver transplant. Nicole was barely 25. "Barely 25? Come on," you might say. "It's not that bad. There are others who lose their parents in infancy." True. By 25, Nicole had a steady job, could provide for herself, and was healthy. But when you put things into perspective, feelings and perspectives are different to a 25-year-old when she loses a parent. As an adult, she quickly realized the things her mom will miss. She won't go to Nicole's wedding, never meet her husband (if she ever finds one), never meet her unborn child, and never see what she made of herself. She'll never cheer her every milestone, take care of her grandchildren, witness them grow, see the new house she'd buy, or experience all the things Nicole did in life. She's just – gone, as if she never existed, like a small wave going unnoticed into the middle of the Indian Ocean.

The last thing Nicole wanted was to miss her flight. She wanted to get out of Bali and knew they had to rush, but she also knew Chloe was very resourceful. She knew how to cut lines, invent excuses, and get their way through security lines much faster. Unorthodox? Yes. But Nicole was nowhere near religious at this point.

"Hey, sunshine," Chloe said suddenly, disrupting Nicole's standstill in the check-in line.

"Hey, sunshine," Chloe insisted, demanding an answer, "Guess what?"

"What?" Nicole replied, playing Chloe's game, annoyed.

"I got us an upgrade."

"What?!"

"First class!"

"That's amazing."

"I'm amazing"

"You're amazing."

"I'm amazing. OK. You're amazing, too. When you cry me a river, it works like a charm."

"Oh, fuck off, Chloe," Nicole replied, then wiped her tears, laughed, and pushed Chloe to the side. She always knew how to get Nicole to snap out of her state of mind.

They boarded a night flight back to New York, but Nicole couldn't sleep. She ordered some red wine and had been resigned to the idea that she'll just stare into the dark space the entire flight, which was packed. After all, it was Christmastime, and the boarding process took forever. However, just as they hit their last call mark, a beautiful woman in her 60s walked in. She had the calmness of old money and the confidence of a self-made millionaire, which was a rare combination and extremely hard to read.

"Good evening," she whispered to Nicole as she placed her Hermes bag on the chair right next to her.

"Good evening," Nicole whispered back, hypnotized by her presence.

"Eva Robinson," she said, then reached her hand toward Nicole, who wasn't used to this kind of airplane interaction and usually was deeply not open to it. But there was something about Eva Robinson's presence that made Nicole reconsider her flight manners.

"Nicole," she replied back, naively, almost like a starstruck schoolgirl.

"Pleasure."

Nicole nodded in approval.

"I'm a terrible sleeper, so if you're up for a wine partner for that red, I'd love to," Mrs. Robinson continued.

"By all means," Nicole smiled.

"How come you're not staying for New Year's Eve?" Mrs. Robinson asked.

"I just want to leave this place."

"Oh, yeah. Too many tourists this time of year."

"Yeah."

Mrs. Robinson looked at Nicole almost like she was fishing for more information. She seemed curious in nature, but she also had that old money look. Old money doesn't ask for information; old money gets what it needs. She turned away, poured herself more wine, and waited.

"It's one year since my mom died," Nicole whispered, almost as a relief they both needed to hear, making Mrs. Robinson turn immediately toward her. "I came to find closure here." Nicole opened her soul to a total stranger, and now she felt a weird sense of vulnerability combined with a rush of relief.

"Oh, honey, I'm so sorry. Can I give you a hug?" said Mrs. Robinson, to which Nicole had no idea how to react. But in moments like this, your mind is silent and hopeless, and won't give you the answers you seek. Your heart, though, will do it all to embarrass you. So, Nicole burst into tears in the arms of a stranger on a first-class flight from Denpansar back to New York.

"Why here?" Mrs. Robinson asked.

"I don't know. Eat Pray Love?" Nicole replied, unconvincingly.

"You don't look the part," Mrs. Robinson replied, waiting for Nicole to fill in the missing dots.

"Perhaps distance."

"Distances and places lose relevance when time no longer matters," Mrs. Robinson replied.

"I was away when it all started, in South Africa, the first time my mom was sent to the ICU. Perhaps, being away from the place it happened brings me back to that short moment of silence before all hell broke loose."

"What happened to your mom?"

"Failed liver transplant."

Mrs. Robinson grabbed her hand and said nothing, as if she knew that anything she'd say wouldn't be what Nicole would need. In return, Nicole didn't resist this stranger's caring gesture and held on to her hand as if it was that one thing she'd been longing for a year. Slowly, steadily, she fell asleep thinking about her mom's green eyes and the ashes of the letter floating into nothingness.

When her mom got sick, Nicole was on the other side of the world, shooting a TV ad for a beer brand on the coast of South Africa. She received a simple text – "Call me, mom is in the hospital" – the most mundane 24-character text that shattered her well-being for the rest of her life. Because that's what life looks like these days. You fall in love, you break up, and you die. And all is announced through an SMS, text, or something extremely ordinary. The ordeal that followed for the next two years was nerve-racking and soul-crushing. Her mom was diagnosed inexplicably and unexpectedly with liver cirrhosis and was in need of an urgent liver transplant. However, liver transplants – any organ transplant, for that matter – aren't easy to come by, no matter where you come from, how rich you are, or where you were born. It was only a coincidence that her family was poor and couldn't pay for that renowned doctor or that state-of-the-art clinic. This time around, not even money would've made a difference.

Since that moment when she found out, Nicole made taking care of mom her life's mission. Her mom was very different, but the trait they both shared inexplicably was resilience. To Nicole, her mom was her superhero. She was her best friend. Her rock. Her therapist. Her everything. She loved her to pieces, and her mom loved her back. They'd talk for hours every day, and her mom always would listen – about Nicole's job, fears, relationships, meeting new guys. Her mom always listened, and listened, and listened. But she never reciprocated, never really opened up her soul. Perhaps that's why Nicole sometimes wondered whether she ever knew her mom the same way her mom knew her. She was the one who did the talking, and her mom did the listening. Never the other way around.

"Was she sick for a long time?" Mrs. Robinson asked without realizing Nicole had fallen asleep. Nicole heard the question, but refused to open her eyes. She pretended she was asleep, distancing her lips just a little bit to mimic more heavy breathing. That wasn't an easy question to answer – not for Nicole and perhaps anyone else who has gone through a similar ordeal. It's probably worth going back to the beginning…

All her life, Nicole had been an impostor. Ever since she was in middle school, she learned the gift of pretending to be someone she wasn't, such as pretending to have a normal family when even as a young kid, it started to become obvious that her family life would be nowhere close to normal. At school, she mingled with different kids from different backgrounds, but most came from the upper middle class or rich families, a consequence of her parents' own making. Nicole's family had the trappings of such a family when she was young, but over the years, they got lost. Well, to be fair, all was lost. They became more unstable financially, lost the house, and were now living in rentals, moving every other month to a new place where they could afford to live, giving her childhood an unsteady roof over her head.

Nicole was ashamed of talking about it, and perhaps it wasn't the kind of discussion kids have during recess anyway, but the thought of not having security creeped in as a young child. She started to become ashamed of bringing friends over to her house, particularly as the houses they moved into became uglier, dirtier, and further away from the city.

Initially, it wasn't that bad, only hitting hard when her parents didn't have the money to send her to summer camp. Even to a small kid, that seemed odd. It took years of her adult life for Nicole to realize where all this was coming from. Initially, she bought into the idea that her parents were unlucky. Gullibly, she believed them when they told her they were cursed, just unfortunate, but it slowly became obvious that the reason behind it was alcohol.

Now, how could she explain to the old money woman sitting in 1A that the reason why she can't open up is because perhaps she shouldn't be in first class in the first place? Uncertainty, shame, and deceit were the values she saw around her house, even though her parents never verbalized them.

Nicole had to carve a space between her heart and her mind, an invisible wall that never allowed the two to collide when it came to her family. Nicole's mind was telling her that she didn't deserve this family, with an alcoholic father, a house she always was embarrassed by, and parents losing control of their lives and never fighting to get it back. It wasn't her fault, and it was unfair. However, her heart told her a different story. Words can't really describe the love they had. Genuine, pure love – proud love. Not the kind you talk about, but the kind that shows. They celebrated their every achievement and suffered with every failure, and yet, was that enough to be a happy home?

Perhaps that's why, when Mrs. Robinson held her hand, it felt genuine. Not the kind of care that's talked about, but the kind of care that's shown. Or perhaps they were just old manners learned over decades with no worries. Whatever the case, there was weird, good chemistry between them.

The plane threw itself to the ground, like an aviation tantrum, or at least that's how it felt to Nicole, abruptly awakening her from her deep sleep as they landed at La Guardia.

"I wish I could sleep like that on planes," Mrs. Robinson told Nicole as she lifted her eye mask and saw the snow covering Terminal B of La Guardia.

"We're lucky they landed in this storm."

"Yeah. Yes." Nicole fixed her sore voice, still confused as to how it was possible for her to sleep the entire fight.

"Where do you live?" Mrs. Robinson asked.

"SoHo."

"Ah," she replied without adding anything else to it. It felt charged with judgment, but Nicole wasn't sure what kind of judgment it was.

"Well, it was great to meet you, Nicole. I hope you find the peace you're looking for."

"Thank you, Mrs. Robinson."

"Please, call me Eva."

"Calling someone by first names requires building trust."

"I love that, Nicole." Mrs. Robinson then smiled.

Mrs. Robinson floated out of the plane as elegantly as she arrived, and Nicole still was mesmerized by her – a gentle old creature who gave her perhaps the comfort she needed to get through that flight home.

"Hey, sunshine, you ready?" Chloe shouted from 3B.

"Yeah. Yes," Nicole responded, still half asleep.

As she walked out of the plane, she started to wonder who Mrs. Robinson actually was. Was she old money? Was she married, and if so, to whom? She took out her phone to Google her, but as with most families of this kind, not even complex algorithms could find the information she needed. Old money is called old money for a reason – they were made way before the Internet. Nicole couldn't help but question the universe again and wonder why she couldn't have a family like that, why life is a matter of geographical and financial luck, a universe's lottery. The only difference was, as Nicole would geek out about often, that you statistically have one in around 13 million chances to win a lottery. However, to be born in a billionaire family, you have one in 27 million chances. Nicole's background was 27 million miles away from that.

Living with an alcoholic parent does things to your soul. Most of the time, it's not abrupt, it's not violent, and you don't read about it in newspapers. Most of the time, it's silent, slow, painful, hopeless torture that eats up your soul. It steals your identity even though you're not the one holding the bottle in your hand. It also raises questions: "Why us?" "Why me?" "What does the world think?" It also elicits guilt in the most unguilty people and makes crying a daily routine and a moment of silence a miracle. It brings some people together and breaks others apart. Alcoholism, though an individual choice, silently becomes a systemic family issue.

Kids with alcoholic parents learn how to hide their families from everybody else. They feel like it's their fault somehow, so they learn how to fake a happy family. Nicole was no exception. If someone didn't know her dad and asked about him, she could dance around the answer like an Olympic dancer. She could talk for hours about the great things he did – and mind you, she wasn't lying about that, but she was only talking about his life before the bottle. He was a very smart man, very educated, from a good family. He graduated magna cum laude and built his own company, which reconstructed museums and heritage centers preserved by UNESCO back in the day. But that was – well – way back in the day, before Nicole even knew basic trigonometry.

Nicole felt like she never actually knew her dad when she actually did know him. There wasn't much left of who he truly was by the time she became a young adult. He was just – a drunk. There really was nothing more there to see, but she always wanted to feel like there was more to it than that, that she just never really knew him. You see, the problem with alcohol is that it doesn't just erase the memory of the one who drinks; it also robs the ones around him from good memories. Nicole didn't remember much about dad – she remembered drunk dad, but not dad before that. Her only fond memories were from when she was maybe 4 years old, and her dad would read stories to her until she fell asleep. Her sensory memories included his mustache tickling her as he kissed her good night, or his cologne as he carried her on his shoulders. That was pretty much it on the bright side, and they all stopped around 8–9 years old. Everything that followed afterward was pure horror.

Nicole soon became a silent witness to a dysfunctional couple and bad parenting. She often found her mom crying while hiding in the kitchen pantry. Other times, she'd miss her dad, who was absent from all the school celebrations, graduations, and birthday parties. Nicole's memories of her dad were vague, but his arrivals were sensorial. They were ingrained in her soul, and to this day send shivers down her spine. She perfectly recalled her dad arriving home from work, at least by his accounts, and the house going quiet in an instant – like crabs burrowing under sand when someone passes by, or how turtles go into their shells when predators approach. When her dad arrived home, everybody would wait to get sight of him and check his mood. Will it be a quiet night or a fistfight? It could be a sigh and a sense of relief if dad was making jokes – or a signal for everybody to retreat to their rooms and be quiet if he was angry. The dog was a great barometer. He was on the front lines and would know in an instant what's to come. If the dog headed for cover, so would the family.

Now, having lived with that and having your mom, not your dad, passing away after a liver transplant, that was pretty ironic. Or at least that's what Nicole still thought, arguably still lying to herself. So, how could she honestly have answered Mrs. Robinson's question of "Was she sick for a long time?" That's not a simple question to answer.

Immigration at La Guardia was a mess, as it always was. When they approached the line, Nicole could spot Mrs. Robinson in front of her, around 10 people ahead. From afar, she now could study her better – her style, demeanor, and personality. There's something just so magnetic about her such that Nicole couldn't take her eyes off of her. She had dark hair and green eyes like her mom, but that couldn't be the reason why she was so drawn to her. Mrs. Robinson saw her and waved. Nicole nodded and looked away, a bit embarrassed that she was caught in the moment of stalking.

"This takes forever. I bet our bags will be off belt by the time we reach them," Chloe said.

"Yeah, but that's not bad though." Nicole secretly continued stalking Mrs. Robinson, who was now past immigration and walking out.

"I wonder who she is," Nicole finally admitted to Chloe.

"A bad-ass woman, that's who," Chloe replied, in her signature style. Nicole nodded and approached the immigration officer, losing sight of Mrs. Robinson, whom she most likely would never see again.

Back home in SoHo, Nicole ordered her favorite noodles from Tanli. She opened a bottle of red wine and poured herself a glass to unwind. She was still shaken, still mourning. One glass became two, one thought became another, and she became restless again, so she decided to close the loop on her emotional journey that night.

She drifted off on her sofa and returned to a dream that kept repeating itself in a different shape or form each time. She was searching for her mom in this deserted, dystopian city. The buildings looked like they had collapsed, and every now and then, from the upper floors' shattered windows, long, white, silk curtains would break through and flutter under the sun's rays, disturbed by a sandy haze. As she watched the curtains dance, she noticed her mom between them, sort of floating, as if she needed to be rescued from a tower in the big unknown. She rushed up the stairs to the last crooked door on the top floor, took a deep breath, and opened the

IMPOSTOR FIGURES

door. Suddenly, a loud noise echoed everywhere, but she couldn't see her mom anywhere now. The incessant noise became louder and louder. Was it the life support machine her mom was connected to, a needle falling to the floor... Suddenly, she awakened to notifications pinging from her dating app. Again and again. Dizzy and annoyed to have missed her mom in her dream, she opened the app. There they were: five messages from a D. Robinson.

"That's the weirdest coincidence," she thought.

Nicole didn't expect much from the dating app, and by this time, she didn't expect much from any date, really. Years of dating while taking care of her mom took a deep toll on her trust, self-confidence, and – quite frankly – her expectations.

She had maybe around eight "meaningful" relationships in the year and a half her mom was awaiting a liver transplant, and each time she met someone, she tried hanging on to them because the comfort and escape she found in the arms of a stranger made her think she had a normal life. Nicole never really talked to any of them about what was going on in her life, hoping that she once again could hide the truth or avoid it, as she did all her life. However, adulthood is different. People wonder, question, then eventually give up trying to understand, and while she never really talked about it, every breakup, every ghosted text, every call left unanswered left her just a little bit more empty. Under normal circumstances, Nicole would lie to herself that she didn't care too much about it. This time around, though, such a long time spent on meaningless dates was too much even for her. Imposture ruins confidence, and she would become a relic soon.

D. Robinson's first picture was the perfect cliche of a rich playboy. A good-looking one, indeed, but a rich playboy nevertheless. She sighed and rolled her eyes, but curiosity made her keep shuffling through the pictures. The more she shuffled, the more she fell into his cliches and the pictures checking the boxes of a dating app. The next pictures were of him diving (adventurous, check), of him and his dog (able to commit, check), and the last one from the series was with him and his family at Christmastime (family man, check). It was definitely a very rich family, as they were all dressed up in front of a giant tree decorated with different shades of red. She looked closer at every person in the picture and suddenly, her heart stopped. She couldn't believe what she saw. Right there, in front of that big tree sitting right next to him, there she was: Eva Robinson in all her majestic glory, wearing a white sweater with a big flower made out of pearls, the kind of festive sweater you don't find in Target's aisles. She looked as stunning as she did when they left Bali. Now Nicole did, indeed, get more superstitious since her mom had passed away a year before, but this was enough of a coincidence for anyone to start questioning the order, or chaos, of the universe.

The messages from D. Robinson said:

"Hi…"

"How are you?"

"Enjoying the app?"

":)"

":))"

Nicole finally replied:

"Hi." Nicole took it slowly, not knowing where to go next.

D. Robinson came online, so she felt obligated to continue.

"You sound like a bot, but your poor use of emojis gives you away as human," she continued.

"Smileys, not emojis. :) :))" D. Robinson replied.

"In a series."

"Best series recommended for you, Nicole."

"OMG. Cringe."

"You're more of a blockbuster. I can see that," D. Robinson continued with the joke.

"Please stop."

"Already? We didn't even get to the climax of the story. OK, I did it. I cringed myself. Let's start over."

Nicole's phone started to vibrate as she was about to text back D. Robinson. "Dad!" appeared on the screen. He probably just wanted to see whether she got home safely, but he was the last person she wanted to talk to. He was always the last person she wanted to talk to. Her dad had no limits or understanding of what's right or what's wrong, so he called again. And again. And a fourth time, hoping she'd pick up. And yet, every time, she didn't. Picking up a call from him was always a chore, an obligation, and after a 22-hour flight, a chore was the last thing she wanted. She carefully placed the phone on the nightstand, with the screen facing down. So slow – as if someone could hear or see the gesture. She turned her back toward it and closed down the light, pretending to fall asleep while her phone was still vibrating, as if her dad could see what she was doing – a habit she developed as a young girl when he'd come home drunk.

Nicole never had a good relationship with her dad, but since her mom died, she despised him. She blamed him and his bad influence over her mom for her passing. In fact, without any remorse, Nicole wished her dad were gone instead of her mom, and many times, she wished her dad never existed, never met her mom, never became her father. Of course, she never verbalized this, as people would view her as a sociopath if she did. Sometimes, as a young adult, she'd tell her mom to divorce her dad and fantasized about how it would've been if her mom had stayed with her high school sweetheart she secretly read about in her mom's teenage diary. Certainly, she'd still be here and would get to see her kids' lives progress. But now her mom will never experience it. Nicole realized the absurdity of these thoughts, but they comforted her, and putting all the blame on her dad allowed her to daydream about how different her life could've been if mom never had met dad.

When you scream, the universe listens. Her dad got cancer six months after her mom passed away. By that time, Nicole was only a shadow of who she once was. Part of it was becoming a different person, part of it was whatever was left from her old self. She somehow managed to get herself up on her feet again, finally met someone whom she was in a relationship with, and just wasn't ready to go through this again. It was as if the universe just entertained the idea of laughing in her face and testing her to see just how much she could take. But her glass was already full, and she finally had some time for herself to empty the final drops that made all her world spill out. So, she went back into her shell and decided not to come out this time around for her dad and decided to be selfish. Thus, she only pretended she cared.

To be fair, her dad only called her when he wanted something, and it was usually money. He was mostly drunk all the time, repeating the same things about his life, so over time, she stopped answering his phone calls. Again and again. She just never had the mental space to chit-chat with a drunk father about things that only make sense to him. Plus, she'd heard all his lame stories before. Why would she care? He never asked her once how she was, if work was all right, if she's eating right – you know, the kinds of annoying things parents ask when they care. She never had that. Her dad was annoying, but not the way she'd want him to be annoying.

The next morning, she awakened with a headache the size of her trip back from Bali. She blamed it on the bad wine from the flight. It was always easier to blame that than to dig down and see whether something else was wrong, even though morning migraines were a pretty common occurrence lately. She dreaded mornings, and the very thought of going back to work, with just a few days remaining until the new year, made her feel anxious.

She picked up the phone and faced the inevitable: nine missed calls from "Dad!" and two notifications from D. Robinson:

"You there?"

"Guess not."

"Hi. Sorry about that. I fell asleep," she texted back and waited, staring at the screen, hoping he'd type back. He didn't. After all, you can't fight the ego of a mama's boy.

"Yo! You up?" A text notification from Chloe suddenly popped up on the screen.

"Yeah."

"Jasmine hooked us up for a few parties over the weekend."

"Not doing it."

"Come on, Grinch. I need you."

"For Jasmine?"

"Welllll – yeah."

"You've been trying to hook up with her since forever. Even I'm bored."

"Fuck you :))"

"Where is it?"

"Madison."

"Hell no!"

"I know. Hear me out. Won't be any ad folks. I've seen the invite. A lot of Wall Street folks."

"I don't know what's worse."

"OK, you're Grinching, but you'll be there. Tomorrow at 9 p.m. I'll email u the details."

Nicole had been mingling with money folks most of her adult life and somehow got herself infiltrated into an exclusive unofficial club of rich people in New York whom, let's be honest, never open their doors to anyone. Perhaps it was because she was very well known in her field of work, or because she had the vocabulary they understand. Maybe she just knew how to deal the cards she was dealt. She didn't go to an Ivy League school, didn't have estates to inherit, no trust fund as a cushion. Her only understanding of what an ETF is came about when she heard jokes about boring investments from Wall Street bros. She stepped into a private jet for the first time when she actually pitched the business of that private jet's maker. Granted, the jet never got off the ground, but it worked as a showroom, a studio for a mediocre ad, and a fake setup for micro-influencers. She wasn't old-money-worthy by any means, but as with most things in life, Nicole knew how to find the key to the castle. Well, maybe this was more of a heist than a legal entrance. She knew there was no way out and that she had to show up for Chloe. After all, she'd just flown around the world with her, but those messages just made the vein on the right side of her temple throb even harder. Another migraine was in bloom.

When your mind's on fire, though, and you journey into the silent darkness of your depression without even realizing it, every event, call, and minute elicit dread. She never truly recovered from her mom passing away, but more so, she never truly considered the heaviness of the year prior to that and the mental state she was in. This time, she wasn't just lying to the world; she was lying to herself. Right then and there, in Apartment 3A somewhere in SoHo, days before New Year's Eve, an unidentified depression started to show its teeth. But without ever noticing, she kept going, brushing it off as the aftermath of a bad year and jet lag.

Two hours later, Nicole was still in bed, watching the curtains move from the radiator that was blasting heat. It was a sunny winter day, and she already could hear tourist chatter in the streets, mostly people racing into shops they can find in most cities of the world to buy things they can find online. She picked up the phone again, looked at Raya, but heard nothing back from him. What if she just spent the day in bed? She pulled down the curtains, closed her phone as a sign of protest against her imaginary nemesis, and collapsed into a day filled with cheesy TV series and junk food. To the rest of the world, this didn't really seem like the kind of person Nicole was – someone who would just let days fly by, staying in bed and hiding from the world. To the rest of the world, she was outspoken, always smiled, and was full of life. However, deep down, Nicole wasn't that person. Perhaps she was an introvert, but she couldn't really recall whether she always had been like this. Was she always an introvert or did she just become one?

A few days later, she inevitably found herself in a penthouse on Madison. Chloe was mesmerized, as she always was, by the presence of Jasmine, whom she had a crush on since university years. This was a party thrown by Patrick, some rich guy from Wall Street as far as Nicole knew, and she had plenty of "Patricks" in her life. So, she had no interest in getting to meet him that day. She looked around the room to try and find an empty seat and some headspace, away from pointless conversations.

"Blanc de Blancs, madam?"

"Why not?" she replied, smiling back politely to the tall waiter with gorgeous green eyes.

"Bored?" An unknown voice suddenly interrupted her moment with the waiter.

"Excuse me?" she immediately replied, turning around to the tall man who just sat next to her.

"Hello, stranger," said Mrs. Robinson's son, sitting right next to her.

Nicole's heart went small, her cheeks red, and sweat suddenly started to break through her skin.

"Ha, the emoji rookie," she mumbled, unconvincingly.

He took a sip of his glass and put on a satisfied smirk as he did that. His generational, confident smirk.

"I like your watch," he said, as he pointed at her vintage Datejust.

"Thank you," she replied, noticing his gold Nautilus – a different league.

Before knowing this world and how it operated, she would've opened a debate about the two watches and how much she loves his, how she got hers, and how one day she hopes to have one just like his. But she knew she couldn't do that. He doesn't need to know that's her only watch, that she'd never seen a gold Nautilus up close before, and most likely, he doesn't care. Bragging about watches screams new money. Or worse, screams no money.

"I'm not sure what's up, but you have something very mysterious that's attractive to me, Nicole."

She smiled, somehow everything he said made her paralyzed with emotion.

"I tell you what. Why don't we have a proper breakfast."

"Breakfast?"

"Yeah. Let's start fresh." he took another sip of champagne, looked at her, and smiled. Such a weird essence emanated from him, his confidence, and his warm face. He had a genuine smile that was impossible to ignore.

"What do you say? Tomorrow at 8.30 at Casa Lavender?"

"8.30?" she said, compelled by his irresistible look.

"Yes. This way we won't stay long tonight."

Nicole smiled.

"Or maybe I just want the morning to come faster." He then finished his drink and placed it on the table. Without even giving Nicole a chance to reply, he got up and left, leaving her behind, stunned. He was such a player, and yet she was totally falling for his game.

"Good night, Nicole," he shouted from afar, without even looking back.

Nicole watched him get lost in the crowd, in awe of how much he resembled Mrs. Robinson. He was tall, handsome, and had the same magnetism she was blessed with. Before he turned the corner, he gave her one last look as if he felt she was watching, smiled, and left the party. After he left, Nicole suddenly lost interest in the party. That was her cue too. She looked at her phone. It was late, and she had five more missed calls from her dad.

"Fuck!" she told herself, annoyed, realizing she'll have to answer or call back tomorrow. Every missed call was an anchor to her dark reality.

When Nicole first met her mom's surgeon, her soul was crushed: Her mom wasn't admitted to the transplant list initially because alcoholics needed to prove sobriety for six months before they got a chance to survive. For many, this was a death sentence, but her mom wasn't an alcoholic, or at least that's what Nicole firmly believed to this day.

"She is not!" she swore to the doctor. Sure, she had the occasional drink, but who doesn't? She's not an alcoholic." She begged the doctor, desperate to find a string to pull for her mom's life, but blood tests don't lie, and doctors don't overwrite ethics. However, her dad was a raging alcoholic, and he exerted an incredible influence over her mom.

After a while, Nicole moved her mom to New York. This way, she would be closer to the best hospitals in the country and far away from her dad. She'd be just a few minutes away when they get the call from the hospital saying they found a liver for the transplant. In the depths of her misery, Nicole never lost hope.

Her mom passed the sobriety test six months later and was up for the transplant. "Of course she did!" Nicole reassured the doctor "I told you, my mom isn't an alcoholic!" and while her heart would scream that toward the entire world, her mind would start to question it.

Over the next year, Nicole was her mom's shoulder. She watched her decay, but she was there 24/7. What nobody tells families of people needing an organ transplant is that their phones never can be on silent, and they can't get on a plane or go where there's no network coverage because if a compatible organ becomes available, you gotta answer that call. This is the one phone call you can't call back, can't let your answering machine pick up, and you can't get a text. This is the one call you pick up, or the organ goes to the next in line. So, Nicole was always on call. She traveled less for work and never entered an underground bar, remote hotel, or concert where cell coverage might by shaky. She took the stairs more often than the elevator. She'd done that for years, so perhaps that's why she now felt she was at liberty to ignore her dad's messages completely and keep her phone on silent.

The morning she was about to meet the emoji rookie, the son of an old money goddess, she decided to take the leap and call her dad first. It was time. The phone rang a couple times, and he answered.

"Hello, honey. Are you OK?" he asked, sounding perfectly sober and normal.

That tone of voice took Nicole back in time, to when she witnessed a miracle. A few months after her mom got sick, she saw a glimpse of what her dad once was when he came to pick her up from the airport. He was lucid, and his eyes weren't wet and blurry. He was smart, funny, stood tall, carried her bag, and drove her home. He was a different person. He was finally *a dad.* He decided to give up alcohol for mom and save her. She finally saw what her mom saw 25 years before when she met him. It was in that moment that Nicole was ready to let it all go, all of it. All the years of sorrow, all the tears, all the blurry moments, the robbing of memories, the panic attacks, the moments of silence, the embarrassment, the lies. All of it, for the slim chance of a second life – or at least the idea of it.

Those days, she could sit down and have a conversation with her dad. He had good jokes, remembered what she said, was reliable, and for the first time in their life together, he actually listened. It was the first time in his life when he wasn't selfish. But you know, miracles only happen once, and as Nicole had seen plenty of times in her life, for the most part, they don't last long, and they pass by unnoticed. However, Nicole noticed it this time, but her dad didn't. He was given a second chance to give up alcohol for his family and for himself. His body wouldn't shiver, and he wouldn't go into withdrawals. His body would accept the fact that alcohol wasn't part of his life anymore. But – he didn't notice, and the miracle soon went away.

"Hi, dad!" she replied to her dad. "I'm all right. Recovering after Bali."

"Oh, hmm, Bali?"

She then realized that the miracle was gone after three seconds.

"Let me tell you who I met yesterday," he continued, completely oblivious to her.

"Dad, I gotta go. You OK?"

"Yes, yes. It was Mr. Wal, Mr. Walt, Mr. Wallace," he mumbled, clearly drunk already.

"Dad, I have to go. Take care."

They say alcohol changes your brain. It kills both your reward centers and your cortex, which define your identity. You morph into someone else, into an identity your old self wouldn't identify with, but which is impossible to escape. Books and exhaustive research have tried to clarify that alcoholics can give up alcohol with the right guidance. Sure, Nicole thought about this many times, but then again, it was all just a theory. Try to explain this to someone who was born into alcoholism, who knew nothing else. Nicole was born into this war, and she never thought she could win it one battle at a time.

She still was feeling tired from the trip, from last night or possibly from life, but she pushed herself off the bed to go to Casa Lavender. There, without ever thinking it'll go that way, her future husband was waiting.

***

Nicole couldn't figure out whether it was an old money thing or just a Robinson family thing, in which girlfriends are introduced to families very late. Six months into the relationship, she still hadn't met his family, but she didn't think about it too much. Or that's what she tried to convince herself. Somehow, whenever someone would ask her whether she's OK with that, she undoubtedly would answer that she is – another behavior she was forced into learning in the years of her life before her mom passed away.

A few months after being admitted to the list, her mom wasn't doing well. She had lost a lot of weight, and Nicole started to lose faith that the phone would ever ring, that her mom would make it, that their lives would be the same again. But there's something weird about illness, whether yours or that of someone around you: It makes you reconsider the very definition of happiness. She realized that this was her mom's last fall on this planet. She was hospitalized in and out for months now, and in a weird, painful way, that fall was magic. The WCU Hospital was in Nicole's head like purgatory, the place where dead people go and wait to see whether they'll go to hell or heaven. Most of the time, getting out was pure sorcery. It was an old U-shaped building with lots of alleys and trees in its yard, which was puzzling because the patients there were too sick to walk around there anyway. The alleys were filled with leaves of all shades and colors, and it was awfully quiet. Nobody was rushing, nobody was talking, nobody was crying. It was pure silence. She walked through that alley every time she dropped her mom off at the hospital. It was a mental vacuum – a place where she could go in, float around, and escape this reality, and have the quickest, yet most profound, conversations with the universe.

She thought many times about how life prepares you for the good struggles – having kids, getting an education, building a family. Everyone's got an opinion about that and will share it with you eagerly. Those are the good struggles. But no one prepares you for the bad struggles – the months of pain and grief, illness, losing a relative or friend, having to hide it all from everybody. Nobody tells you about that. Nobody tells you that you have to be careful in life that you don't become a sad person – one who only cries – because you don't want pity or help. You just want to move on, so you gotta fake it. Yet again, Nicole was on that path of pretending she's someone else – a happy person, an ongoing fighter, a fountain of strength and willpower. She was telling everyone she was OK, but inside, she was collapsing.

A 1971 study by Brickman and Campbell (1971) on happiness adaptability that she read once hypothesized that people can relate to a feeling of happiness lived only in the previous three months. So, the concept of happiness is relative, short-lived, and fluid. Our understanding of it was a total fraud, a social construct. Therefore, the very hypothesis that paralyzed people can't be happy could be wrong. Nicole didn't know how accurate these studies were, but it explained why she always reassured people that she was OK when she wasn't. Perhaps it was pure science. Perhaps she wasn't lying to anyone. Maybe it was truth – hard truth, but truth.

She contemplated suicide a couple times, but not in the sense of actually doing something, but more like passing by a bridge and thinking: What if I jumped? Would people notice? Would someone care? Will all this be over? She remembered, though, when she was young that one of her mom's friends killed herself. Pills. That's all they told her. Everybody said that it was an act of a coward to leave everything behind. Such a stupid, old-fashioned thing to say. But now, she thought – what about her? What about how she felt? Isn't the world a little selfish to ask her to be miserable just so that the world is happy, just so she does what's right? Maybe the woman felt she just can't take it anymore, that it wasn't worth it, that every day was the same. Depression is a very dark tunnel that's difficult to escape.

If anybody knew what was going on inside Nicole as she stood in the middle of the bridge near her apartment, looking at the cars passing below on the highway, they would intervene. But she always was smiling. No one would think that a woman as sociable, successful, and beautiful as her ever could consider suicide.

"I mean, there are others who have it worse, Nicole!" they'd say.

"This, too, shall pass."

"Man up."

"Yes, you can do it."

Nicole learned to say "I'm OK," but every time she replied with "I'm OK," an earthquake would move all her thoughts and feelings and make them fall into the depths of her unconsciousness even more. Every "I'm OK" was an 8.3 magnitude earthquake on her feelings scale, the kind of earthquake you hear about on the news, when nothing can be done and everything collapses over what life used to be before. One big earthquake, then a couple of aftershocks would soon hide what was really going on in her head completely.

It was just months after this state of mind, after this deep depression, when she met D. Robinson, her partner she was madly in love with who still hadn't introduced her to his family. And yet – she was OK. One day, she'll meet the family, though she already met Mrs. Robinson. She was an introvert who learned to be an extrovert, and by the time you pass your 30s, you don't always feel like going above and beyond to meet new people. So, while it felt like he wasn't serious about the relationship, she didn't necessarily feel like she wanted to meet his mom right away anyway. And, as with all things in life, they happen when you least want them or expect them.

The day she officially met Eva Robinson was just as ordinary as the day she met her for the first time on the flight back from Bali. It was a gorgeous Saturday, around noon, and D. Robinson was meeting Nicole at City Hall Park for lunch, as she'd spent her morning at the office nearby working on a pitch, a regular occurrence for her. They wanted to try something new besides Casa Lavender, so they tried a new brunch place near Park Row that one of his favorite concierges was raving about. But, as with so many places in New York, having a concierge is not always enough to get into the best places in town. Sure, it can get you close to it, but you still needed to wait for a table. As they waited in the beautiful warmth of an April sun, she noticed from afar a presence with which she was weirdly familiar. It was an energy she could feel – a presence that can't be unnoticed. Floating through the city chaos on Park Row was Eva Robinson. Dressed in a gorgeous, oversized pink Merino suit, she carried herself and her two fawn Whippets, Arnold and Lily, gracefully. Nicole's heart started racing, faster and faster, stronger and stronger, anticipating the inevitable encounter.

"Mom?" D. Robinson yelled from the line.

"Sit," Eva Robinson told her whippets, with no emotion, no grand gesture – just calmness as she turned toward them.

D. Robinson gave his mom a kiss on the right cheek.

"It's a great restaurant. You'll love it," Eva Robinson said.

"I can't compete with you."

"I've been around the block for too long," she retorted, discreetly scanning the line from behind her big black Thome Browne glasses to see whom he was with.

"Come – I want you to meet someone."

D. Robinson grabbed her arm gently, and they walked toward Nicole, whose heart was beating out of her chest.

"Mom, this is Nicole. The love of my life."

As if seeing Eva Robinson in front of her wasn't enough, hearing those five words to introduce her was enough to make Nicole weak in the knees and about to collapse. But Eva Robinson was too intimidating for Nicole's fight-or-flight sense not to kick in.

"Oh, wow, now that's an introduction..." Eva said, stopping in front of Nicole and smiling.

"...Though I have this feeling we've met before," she continued.

"Me too," Nicole continued, leaving herself space for the benefit of the doubt.

"I'm Eva."

"I'm Nicole."

Eva Robinson smiled, as if she remembered, but said nothing.

"Do you want to join us for lunch, mom?"

"Oh no, I don't want to intrude, and Arnold would hate me anyway. I promised we'd go chase grasshoppers in the park. Perhaps next time," she said while looking at her skinny dog.

"All right, mom."

"Enjoy lunch!" she said, then floated away, but perhaps as a signature of the Robinson family, after a few steps, as she passed by Nicole, she gently and discreetly turned toward her and whispered : "I'm glad to see you happy now."

In that moment, almost like that touch from the hand of a stranger on a flight from Denpasar to New York, those few words made Nicole's eyes immediately water. Eva Robinson remembered her too. She was speechless, a deer in the headlights, realizing that the car coming full speed ahead was actually a fuzzy cloud filled with compassion.

"Did you say something, mom?" D. Robinson yelled after that.

"Enjoy lunch!" she repeated from afar.

"Ah, yes, thank you."

"I guess the cat's out of the bag now," he turned to Nicole.

"Your mom is a goddess," she replied.

He smiled, knowing she totally was.

"Did you mean it that you feel like you've met before?"

"I did. I think she sat next to me on my flight back from Bali."

"Oh, I actually thought it was from my Raya profile," he said, then smiled conspicuously.

Nicole smiled back, and they decided to leave it there, suspended in the unknown. Sometimes, the unknown is more than enough knowledge.

"She just texted me and invited us for dinner tomorrow evening. You ready for it?"

"I guess there's no escape now." Nicole then smiled and immediately started to think about what she would wear at potentially one of the most important dinners of her life.

Nicole always thought that when it came to pretending to be wealthy, you needed to know all the wines of the world, be a pro at taking snails out of shells, pair wine with oysters, know how to ride a horse like at the Olympics, and have a concierge to dress you for the occasion, but if you also happen to know how to change a broken pipe under your sink or how to paint a wall, you're not wealthy. You're new money – rich at best, but not wealthy. Somehow, Nicole always gave herself away like that. Sure, it wasn't fixing a broken pipe, but it could be stuff like how to glue a shoe sole or how to remove a wine stain from silk. That Sunday night, she was about to take her final exam.

Sure, D. Robinson knew she wasn't old money, and that she's self-made, but some parts about her past remained a mystery. To be fair, he never bothered to dig deep into that information anyway. He knew that her mom passed away, that they lost everything when she was young, and that she doesn't have a good relationship with her dad, but he didn't know the extent of it all. As for Eva Robinson, she knew nothing about Nicole. The only thing she knew is that she travelled first class and went to Bali to find herself after her mom's death, but that was it. What if she thought she was also old money too? What if she sees through her? What if by next week, she intervenes in their relationship, and it all will be over? She was terrified.

That night, Nicole told D. Robinson she wanted to sleep at her place under the pretense that she still had some clothes to pick up from there and had to finish up a project for work, so they can have all of Sunday together. In reality, though, she knew it was far-fetched and odd to him that she actually just wanted to go shopping for this very important meeting. She was about to make an investment in the most understated Tom Ford dress she'd seen a few months before, but never actually wanted to pay the price. That Saturday, she was ready to make an investment in her future. It had the right balance between luxury and understated branding, that "if you know, you know" style. She placed the dress on a velvet hanger and poured herself a big glass of red. She was so stressed out, she needed some help to sleep. She felt like a schoolgirl before her first day of school after the holidays.

Eva Robinson lived in the West Village in a gorgeous three-story brownstone house in NoLita. It seemed contrary to what Nicole was expecting, as she imagined someone like her would be living in a brownstone house somewhere between East 67th and 69th, or near it. But she was nothing like what Nicole had expected. Her house didn't contain any big chandeliers, old furniture, tall ceilings – nothing that screamed old money. Quite the contrary. Her home was newly decorated, with simple white walls and a beautiful blue velvet sofa that dominated the living room. A combination of dark smoked wood and marble made the house feel homey, yet intimidating to rookies. That's how she was.

"Welcome!" Eva Robinson greeted them herself. "Champagne?"

"Sure!" Nicole answered, trying to be as natural as possible.

Eva Robinson served the champagne herself and handed Nicole a glass.

"You look really pretty, Nicole!"

"Thank you."

Let's sit down. Gabriela will help us out.

"Gabriela!" D. Robinson yelled with excitement and ran toward a short, kind-looking woman, somewhat the same age as Eva Robinson, and gave her a big hug.

"Gabriela is my help, my son's second mom, and, well – she's family."

"Nice to meet you, Gabriela."

"Likewise, senorita. I can see why my boy's crazy for you."

"OK, let's sit. Tell me all about yourself, Nicole."

"All right, take it easy, straight-shooter," D. Robinson shouted from the kitchen, with mouth half full, rummaging through a jar of nuts and trying to get the last pecans at the bottom of it. Eva Robinson smiled and said nothing in her defense, leaving some space for Nicole to actually answer.

"Well, I don't know what you know about me."

"Well, obviously nothing," she said, pointing at her son, who had kept her hidden and was smiling again.

"She's a successful advertising executive born in Boston and living in New York. We met at a party at Patrick's," he said, then looked at Nicole and winked.

"Pattrick! How is Pattrick? I haven't seen him in years."

"Well, he's the same. Just richer."

Eva Robinson smiled and turned back to Nicole, lifted her eyebrows, and rolled her eyes. She clearly didn't really like Pattrick and neither did Nicole.

"Well, good for him," she answered back and winked at Nicole, helping her loosen up a bit.

"What brought you to New York, Nicole?"

"Well, my job. I got an offer here, rose up the ladder, and never looked back."

"Mhmm, and do you like it?"

"Well, I don't know anything else to do, so I have to like it."

"We spend a third of our lives working, a third sleeping, and a third living. So yes, it's important as we have pretty limited time."

Eva continued: "And your dad? Is he in New York as well?"

"No, he's in Boston.'"

"It's just an hour flight. It's OK."

"Yeah. It's not that bad."

"Well, next time we should invite him to dinner too. What do you think, Gabriela?"

"Si! The more the merrier."

Nicole smiled, but her heart stopped for a second. There's no way she could bring her dad to meet Eva Robinson. There's no way she could bring her dad to meet anyone. Period. How could she introduce her dad to Mrs. Robinson? The horror. How could she place a drunk in front of this beautiful woman, dressed in Chanel from head to toe? Where could her dad fit in this picture, and how would she not be taken out of it when they found out? It was the first time that Nicole's game was being threatened by reality. She played this dangerous game for years, in which she pretended that her family was normal and only vaguely would say she doesn't have a great relationship with her dad. But that's pretty much where the conversations stopped. Abruptly. She never mentioned why they were estranged and never created opportunities for questions.

"I'll think about it," Nicole unsurprisingly answered.

"They don't have a great relationship," D. Robinson added, already accustomed to her answer. Granted, he already met her dad a few months earlier and understood the ordeal.

"Oh, we all fight with our parents. Everything can be fixed," Eva Robinson replied with calm, unspoken curiosity.

Well, it was this calm at family gatherings that made it the most awkward for Nicole. It was the warmth, the nonchalance, that just made everything worse. The parent remarks, the silly questions like "When will you have a baby?" or "Has he proposed?" were the ones that made Nicole regret not having a family the most. She always was fascinated by how people who had a family didn't realize the privilege they had. She never understood how some people just take family bonds for granted. Nicole never got any of those questions, as her dad never did something for her, and to be honest, he never really cared.

Nicole's secret about her parents was embedded in her DNA and kept mutating. She still carried the guilt she felt as a child for her parents' poor choices. Even now, as a successful woman in her 30s, she still carried that shadow with her and still didn't let go. While others would stand proud, talk about their past, and revel in being life veterans, she was hiding, scared, and didn't want to have anything to do with the life before she became who she was today. Nicole's dad was her best-kept secret. Bringing him to a dinner in New York would've been the first time her past and future needed to collide, and perhaps this time, all she actually could do, if she really wanted a life with D. Robinson, was to brace for impact.

You'd think that her dad could just stay sober for a few hours and play the normal-dad card. Unfortunately, you can't book time with alcoholism. It's a 24/7 kind of commitment. Nicole knew that if this encounter ever occurred, there was nothing – no preparation – nothing that would stop dad from being, well – drunk dad. She'd seen this before in tougher times, and he didn't change. When her mom was in the hospital and he showed up, it was embarrassing. He didn't know what he was supposed to do or how to help. At times, it didn't even feel like he wanted to help. He was unreliable, egotistical, the true definition of a drunk. He wasn't there to give a helping hand, just talk nonsense, be embarrassing, and remain in denial about the real situation. This dinner invitation would lead to nothing else.

The night at Eva Robinson's continued uneventfully. Hard to beat an impending catastrophic event anyway. It felt slightly like an out-of-body experience for Nicole, watching from afar the Robinson family's laughs and kisses as she was foreseeing, or perhaps manifesting, the worst yet to come. There's no escape from that encounter. It was either that or her relationship with D. Robinson. And, well, according to Nicole, whatever the path, the consequences would be similar. So, she slowly went inside her shell, turning that first encounter into a disaster as she just wasn't able to get out of her shell again. She had prepared for that moment, that meeting with Eva Robinson for so long, and yet, she chose to ignore the elephant in the room completely – her own family and the contrast to the life she aspires to have.

It's not easy climbing the social ladder in New York, and when it comes to old money, she knew there's no ladder to climb. They had elevators with access keys. No key, no entrance.

"You should go see your dad," D. Robinson said as they drove back home.

"Yeah. Yes."

"I mean it," he insisted, not turning around to face Nicole and almost sounding slightly like he had issued a weird threat.

Nicole sat there, looking into the abyss of the Brooklyn Bridge as they crossed over to Williamsburg. She was numb. D. Robinson took his right hand off the steering wheel to hold her hand, almost as a gesture of empathy, though he wasn't famously known for it. He turned his head, looked at her, and smiled.

"Come on, why the long face? All will be well."

Nicole turned to him and smiled. He leaned over, kissed her on the cheek, and opened the glove compartment without her even noticing. He pulled out a small box and placed it on her knees.

"I mean it," he insisted again and turned his gaze back to the road.

Nicole looked at the small velvet box on her knees and knew what was inside, but it just didn't make any sense. Zero. It was a bad day, a bad dinner, a bad encounter, and she came from the wrong past. She was an impostor. How? Why? Now what? She looked at it for a few seconds that felt like an eternity before she opened it up to face the beautiful inevitable.

"Are you serious?"

"It's quite rare that I am."

"You're mad."

"Music to my ears."

Nicole pulled out the ring and put it on her finger. It was a beautiful square yellow diamond ring that reflected the lights of New York in ways that she never dreamed possible.

"So?"

"I'm in shock."

"I insist,"

"OK."

"OK?"

"OK."

"Now that's a proposal!" D. Robinson ironically remarked, and they both burst into laughter. "You're the first girl I ever brought home, and I always said the first girl I bring home will be the first girl I marry."

"The *first* girl."

"Precisely," and he laughed again.

"Jerk. It's beautiful."

"I'm glad you like it. Now stop with the long face. All will be well."

For a short moment, Nicole forgot about it all. The night, the date, her dad, the impossible mission ahead of her.

***

There's no escape from facing the inevitable. She had to tell her dad she's getting married, confront their past, brief him, and fake normality for just one day. Well, two: the day he'll meet Eva Robinson and the day she gets married. However, that conversation required more than a phone call or text – she had to travel back home.

Going home was always an emotional rollercoaster. Unlike what others would expect, it wasn't because entering the house she grew up in would bring back memories because she didn't have one house she grew up in, and she never lived in the apartment where dad currently was living in. It was a rollercoaster because facing realities always made her ponder about what-ifs.

The road home brought back memories inevitably, though. She was back amid places she explored as a kid, before all hell broke loose in her family. The journey reminded her of car trips they'd take before her parents lost all control of their lives – picnics near rivers, the mountain view, the air, the way the sun set on the hills around her. It's a feeling she felt in her gut. That road was always something she enjoyed.

Nicole never really thought much about the fact that ever since her mom passed away, she always slept in a hotel when she went back home. It wasn't because she wouldn't want to be in the same house where mom used to live. That house was long lost to the bank. She just hated the house and the mess her dad was living in. It was a mirror of the wreck he had been for years, so every time she visited, she stayed at a hotel. This time was no different.

Every time she entered her dad's place, there was a nuclear bomb inside her soul, but not the effects of it. It was right before it hits the ground, when your life flashes before your eyes – when, inside the panic and madness, you can spot details, places to hide, directions to run to, and all this is happening in a split second. Every time. That was the feeling. As she walked into her dad's house, in the midst of her own Hiroshima, she saw her dad sitting in his messy living room in an apartment that her late grandma always tidied up. He was smoking a cigarette and drinking vodka. Not scotch, not whisky. Vodka. She always thought that was the worst kind of alcoholism. The worst of the worst.

From what she knew, this man still was battling cancer. Of course, "battling" was a misuse of the term and an insult to those actually fighting. He couldn't care less and had been in denial his whole life. Or perhaps he just wanted to die. For many years, he lied about his true condition so that he could continue to drink and smoke. Her dad was a shadow of himself – a skinny man with unbrushed hair, untied laces, and blurry eyes. He didn't look happy to see her and was just embarrassed with himself. He knew how she felt, but it was too late for him. It was at that stage in his life when his embarrassment had spread together with the cancer throughout his body. It had metastasized, and there was no turning back now. He looked like he came to terms with who he had become and what was coming and didn't want his daughter to see him this way. To Nicole, that always destroyed her.

She always felt like she should do more, that if only she would've done more, he would've been saved and be a different person, becoming the father she always wanted and never had. But like Hiroshima minutes before, that impact had happened. The blast had settled, and it was now just dark and quiet, amid the smell of death. Her dad didn't want to be saved. It was as if he just wanted to stop existing, just disappear. That always broke her heart and made her angry because it felt like his giving up was proof that she never actually mattered to him. She entered the room and sat down on the couch with him, trying to have a conversation, pretending everything around her was normal. Maybe if he hadn't been the authority figure he once was, if this family would speak their minds more openly, she would ask her dad, "How the hell can you live like this?" "Get up and save yourself" "Let's clean this place up" "Let me put you in a better place." But time had shown that her dad was unsavable, or at least that's what she would tell herself again and again.

Every time she drove home, she hoped to have a decent conversation with her dad and her perceptions would change, that things would change. But it took just minutes for her to realize that this wouldn't happen. Her dad was the same dad that only called when he wanted money and never asked how she was. What broke her heart was the belief that he really cared for her, really loved her, but was too proud to express what he felt.

Her inner torment always would pause with the need to look at old pics, so after a couple of minutes of that, she would ask where the photo albums were and start rifling through them, almost as a desperate call to find a glimpse of normalcy in her past. But every time she looked through old pictures, she realized where she came from. A force within her kept telling her she had to belong to a place where she never fit in.

She realized right then and there that she had an emotional trauma that she constantly wanted to run away from – anger over being a misfit, a sense of wrong that needed to be made right, and a desperate need for justice in front of a court of law that only existed in her imagination.

She always looked for a home she never had, for a feeling she never found. As she drove back home, she loved the feeling of belonging, but as soon as she got there, she wanted to escape from it all, just like she did years earlier. She couldn't save her alcoholic father and couldn't get back the love she never had, the attention she never got. She was in constant need of love and constantly running away from everything that her past was. Nothing could really stop her.

As she shuffled through her childhood memories, she started to notice a glass in mom's hand in a lot of pictures. She remembered her mom having a small glass of vodka every day. Sure, it didn't come in the same size as her dad, and she was listening, wasn't angry all the time, wasn't absent, and was cheerful, loving, caring, and accessible. Unfortunately, surviving has nothing to do with your personality. The universe doesn't favor nice people and only punish bad guys. Your body's own power always supersedes that of your own destiny.

"Dad, are you OK?" she finally asked.

"Well, I'm still alive, if that's what you're asking."

"That's not what I'm asking."

"But what do you want to hear?"

In all honesty, Nicole didn't want to hear a thing. She didn't want to be there in the first place, never mind hearing her dad whining. But this time, she had come by choice, and there was no escape from it.

"I want to know how you're feeling."

"I'm fine. These doctors, they don't know what they're talking about. I'm fine."

"What did they say?"

"Who knows. I stopped going to them. They don't do anything useful anyway."

"Dad, you have to get tests done. You have cancer."

"I don't have cancer. It's gone. I tested, and it's gone."

Nicole knew for a fact that this was just not possible, but by now, she had lost the power to push him to fight for his life. In reality, her dad didn't want to live anymore. He had become some estranged from everyone that he just didn't want to be around no more. He knew he had no one to care for him. So, Nicole knew that there was absolutely nothing she could do, and a big part of her thought that if he'd stay away, it would be better for everyone. Of course, she couldn't admit that.

"OK, dad."

He smiled at her as if both in an act of full lucidity and honesty knew what was coming.

"Dad, I'm getting married."

"Wow. OK. I'm so happy for you."

"Thank you."

"I can't come, Nicole."

"Dad..."

"Look at me. I can't."

"Yes, you can." Nicole started crying for the first time in their father-daughter relationship.

"No. I won't embarrass you. You can tell them I'm sick. Well, I am sick," he laughed.

Nicole hugged him really hard. He smelled like cheap vodka, tobacco, dust, and sweat – a homeless man with a roof over his head.

As she drove back to the airport, the same scenery she saw on the way home changed. The trees weren't as pretty and the sunset not as magical – all of it vanishing in her self-constructed memory of what her childhood once was. All that was left was reality and a sense of abandonment. That was the last time she'd ever see her dad alive, and somehow, she knew it.

***

She didn't like Timothy too much, and by all accounts, a 32-year-old not liking a 7-year-old kid wasn't just weird, but perhaps problematic. But she really didn't like Timothy. Not because of his personality, or his amazing talent in tennis that she didn't have, or because he spoke too loud or threw tantrums in the middle of the court, but because his grandpa took him to classes every day. It was this weird coincidence that made young Timothy wonder why Nicole never liked him. She met Timothy every time she went to the court, and every time she walked on it, her eyes immediately darted toward the grandpa cheering for Timothy from the bench, and she would sigh. She didn't get that, and her kids will never get it either. She was now an orphan. An adult orphan, but an orphan nevertheless.

She missed the idea of a dad – one she never had. She looked at older people and thought of how her parents could've been, how they could've grown old together, their backs curving a little, holding hands, picking up their grandchildren from school, cooking Christmas dinners, and just getting really old and gray. There's a blessing in seeing your parents get old that few realize, she often thought. The life cycle is a blessing, seeing those around you flourish, live out their lives, and slowly fade away. It's natural, normal, and beautiful.

Being an orphan is difficult, no matter the age. Even as an adult, when your parents go too quickly, you still get a feeling of emptiness that can't be filled. There's a way of things that shouldn't be disordered. You become an adult, you have kids, your parents get old, they help you raise your kids, your kids grow up, you get old, your parents pass, you help your kids raise their kids, etc. There's a life passage. When that passage is interrupted, things break within you. It's like a neural network of emotions just suddenly breaks. That's what she always thought. It's electro-shocked and can't truly be restored to factory settings.

When her mom died, Nicole learned about resilience, hidden powers, love, the need to live every day as if it was her last, and doing everything in her power to live the life she dreamed of. When her dad died, she learned about forgiveness, the importance of adaptation, the need to reinvent herself constantly, and the need to move on and keep moving. She learned about not giving up, but death is a sneaky ninja: It sneaks in and, without you noticing, teaches you lessons you never asked for or thought you'd be willing to learn.

For Nicole, unlike when her mom passed away, with her dad gone, her seven stages of grief were all messed up. She didn't have this sort of epiphany when you just forgive and forget, when you wipe away history and remember only the good things, even though that's what the priest advised me to do at the funeral. And it wasn't just about her dad, or denial, anger, bargaining, depression, and acceptance. It was everything all at once.

She started with acceptance, skipped denial and bargaining, then moved directly to anger. She was angry – not at life, destiny, or the universe doing her wrong. She was angry at her parents – really, really angry. She was angry that they didn't take care of themselves, remain alive for the long haul, think about their actions' consequences, or care that they were leaving her and her future behind. Thus, for many months, she didn't feel like an orphan, but actually felt abandoned on purpose. She felt like a foundling. Then anger quickly became depression, which is an ugly monster that feeds on people's silence. The more you don't tell people what you're going through, the stronger the monster gets.

Nicole was very depressed at that time. Thoughts of suicide were no stranger to her since her mom was sick, but this time around, she loved the world around her too much to start entertaining those thoughts. And because you can't hate and love yourself simultaneously, she decided that the whole question of whether she should live or die made no sense. Thus, she resorted to the occasional drink.

The wedding was off by this time, of course. Mrs. Robinson thought it would be inappropriate. Nicole felt a feeling of relief that she now could have a proper wedding, but of course, she could never talk about that with anyone. As her life was shaking again beneath her feet, she felt exhausted, and although she kept telling herself and the world around her that she's OK, she was also afraid she was transforming into what her parents were – hidden, functional alcoholics. Nicole loved her glass of wine, but it was always social, in the company of others, when she went out. She never drank at home alone – ever. That was something she would blame herself for if she did, but over time, it started to feel like she lost control. She felt like after two drinks, alcohol was taking over her mind and behavior. She would forget things the next day and get depressed. Whenever she felt down, she wanted a drink, but admitting to it? That will never happen. Was she becoming her parents?

Alcoholism in this day and age among people is glamorous. It's a social thing. Drinking daily is coping. Getting wasted, and forgetting last night is a good time on a Saturday night. Doing blow every once in a while is high society. So, was she an alcoholic or just a socialite? Among her circles, Nicole's addiction was coming across as letting loose, blowing some steam, so nobody noticed. Not even D. Robinson.

That morning, she awakened, and the room was spinning. It was something she got used to on a Sunday morning, but this time around, it seemed out of the ordinary. Memory fragments of the party they'd been to Saturday night crept in – conversations, stares, the people she hated (who surely saw her wasted, so she'll be the talk of the town now). Oh, and her husband – they had a fight about life, then had crazy makeup sex – again – in someone else's bedroom. Was it protected sex? She can't remember. They must have. A sharp migraine was making her confused anyway. The shame! The shame of not remembering! The same again and again. She dragged the duvet over her head, reached out for an ibuprofen from her nightstand, and went back to bed. Who had she become? A person with a six-day week because the seventh is always spent in bed mourning for her sanity and health, governed by the worst headache and nausea a human being can have. Why was she doing it?

"Do you need anything, honey?" her husband asked, which now had become a regular occurrence on Sunday mornings. Other families had family breakfasts, went for runs in the park, or went brunching and had mimosas at noon. For Nicole, the mere thought of a mimosa would make her want to throw up.

"No. Just gonna sleep here for another hour."

She once read a newspaper story about a guy who was so drunk when he woke up, his house had been broken into. Someone stole the TV he was watching before he fell asleep with a beer in his hand. He woke up the next morning and the only thing remaining was the pillow under his head. So, what did the guy do when he realized where alcohol had taken him? When he realized he had reached rock-bottom? He went to the fridge and cracked open another beer.

A pressure started to build in her chest, and her stomach started to make funny noises. Cold sweat was coming out of every possible pore of her body and a sudden urge to throw up came out of nowhere. Limping, dizzy, and in her hangover fog, she rushed to the bathroom to let it all out.

"You gotta stop drinking, babe. Seriously, it's not good for you," her husband screamed from the other room, an otherwise casual occurrence. It's not that it was jeopardizing their relationship or their life, really, but from where he stood, it would make her too sick, and it just stopped making sense. Nicole always could find excuses as to why she ended up in a situation like the previous night.

"I know, babe. It was a hard week at work, though. We're almost done with that pitch. You know how it is."

"Yeah," her husband mumbled, as if he wasn't in the mood to fight with her about it. "Last night was fun, though, no?" he continued.

"I guess." Nicole struggled to keep it short.

"You seemed like you had a good time," he whispered with a fun tone as he entered the bedroom.

"Did I? I can hardly remember half the night. I feel so embarrassed. Did I make a fool of myself?" she asked, hiding her face covered in mascara and makeup that she hadn't removed before she went to sleep.

"No, I don't think so. Everyone was drunk anyway."

"Seriously, I don't know how you are so in shape right now. Aren't you sick or something?"

"Eh, I have a bit of a hangover, but I'm good. I'll go fix us something to eat. It's 2 p.m. You should get up."

Nicole got up and pushed the button near her bed to open the curtains. The rays of that sunny Sunday and the joy pouring in from the other side of the Hudson River were so out of sync with what she felt that she decided to stop the curtains in their track, just enough to leave a bit of light so she could put on some pants and carry herself to the living room couch. Here she was, she thought to herself, a woman in her mid-30s, one of the five women to watch, according to FW magazine, looking disgusting, lying in her own misery on a Sunday afternoon from her million-dollar apartment in New York. Glamorous indeed. Flashbacks of her dad mixed with yesterday evening's embarrassment and nausea, hitting her in the gut. After crawling all the way to the living room, thinking she had become her dad, the doorbell suddenly rang.

"Did you call somebody over? Tell me you didn't." Nicole ran to her husband fixing lunch in the kitchen.

"No, I didn't," he said, dropping a pan on the oven and heading toward the door. Nicole ran to the bedroom to hide and listened to see who was at the door.

"Oh, OK. Oh, OK. Thank you," she heard her husband mumbling, surprised, then shutting the door. "Nicole! It's for you."

Nicole's heart froze. She looked at herself quickly in the mirror at the wreck she had become.

"Who is it?" she screamed nicely, as she didn't know what to expect.

"It's a box, Nicole."

"What?" Nicole yelled, surprised, and walked into the living room, almost sobering up from the surprise. "A box?"

"Yes. There's a note in it. It's from your cousin."

"My cousin? What cousin?" Nicole was more confused than the moment she opened her eyes that morning. As she stepped into their sunny living room, indeed, she saw her husband holding what seemed like an old box that her cousin from her father's side sent her. Unaware of what this was, she sat down and opened it. The box seemed heavy. She grabbed some scissors and cut away the tape on it. As she opened it, she noticed it was full of papers – letters, notes, pictures. On top of them was a note from her cousin.

"*Dear Nicole,*

Hope this finds you well. This is a box your dad left with us when he moved houses for the last time. He wanted to save them and was afraid they would get lost. I can't store them anymore, and I thought you might want them, I'm sure he'd want you to have them. Come by our place next time you're in town. Susie and Brad are 8 already.

Best,

Michael."

Who was Susie and Brad? Ah, his kids. Now she remembered. The box contained dozens of letters between her mom and her dad, and between her parents and their friends, as well as letters from Nicole as a kid to her mom and pictures of her parents as students. Inside that box was the side of her parents that she had never seen, a part of her childhood she had forgotten about – the good part. She randomly picked a letter from the box – a note from her mom to her dad from the hospital after she gave birth. *"Nicole is so sweet. I love her."* Letters from her parents to their friends back in the day showed how different they were. *"They had friends! They were so fun,"* she screamed to her husband. Her hangover suddenly disappeared, and she sobered up. It was as if it was an intervention from above sent her way, the kind of stuff you see in movies. Dozens and dozens of letters containing jokes and reminiscences of good times, and pictures filled with joy and love showing Nicole the face of her family she had to see and wanted to treasure. This filthy old box was possibly the greatest possession she now had, the single most important thing she inherited from her parents.

Chapter 5

Olivia

When Olivia walked into any room, it was filled with whispers – whispers, not gossip, as there's a difference between the two. Whispers are good, charged with positivity. Gossip is bad, generated by envy – by evil. Olivia was a tall, skinny, dark-haired woman whose faults were hard for anyone to catch. She was the perfect combination of Penelope Cruz and Charlize Theron, probably including their acting skills as well. She knew how to walk, how to talk, how to sit down, and how to stand up for herself, even if she didn't always mean it. She was the very definition of #fierce and #futureisfemale, though she hated anything that had to do with hashtags and self-proclaimed female empowerment.

She was one of the first women to arrive at *FW* to be interviewed for the Five for the Next Five issue. When she got out of the elevator on the 38th floor and stepped into the reception area of *FW*, she needed no introduction. Her blue-flowered Dior coat and red Jimmy Choos were already her signature look. To the amateur eye, it may have seemed like this wasn't her first time at *FW* and definitely not the first interview with Flavia. But strangely enough, it was.

"Olivia!" Flavia's assistant greeted her with enthusiasm. "Welcome. Let's get you settled in for makeup and recording." She pointed toward a room where a makeup artist was waiting for her.

"I won't be needing makeup, thank you." Olivia politely declined the offer.

"Let's talk to the photographer; he might need to do a little retouching," the assistant insisted, already with a step inside the room where everyone was waiting.

"No, thank you." Olivia then turned around and looked to see where the interview actually would be conducted. At the end of the hallway, on the right side from the reception desk, she noticed a camera crew setting up the interview gear into a big airy office.

"We gotta fight that shiny forehead," Flavia's assistant chuckled, discouraged, figuring she already had lost Olivia's interest, as she was already on her way toward the airy room, as if she reigned over this foreign territory.

"If you really don't want to…" she ran after Olivia.

"I really don't want to. Can I get some water?"

"Umm, yes. Right away."

"Sparkling, please."

"Flavia will be with you in just a few moments."

Flavia Wild was one of the best journalists in New York City. She's worked at all major local publications, but after her last stint at the *Times*, she wanted to do her own thing. She's the founder of *FW* and a legend for her powerhouse interviews. She had interviewed everyone from Oprah to the Dalai Lama, and by all measures, Olivia was anxious about this interview. It was a big deal.

FW's headquarters were on the Lower East Side, facing the river and Williamsburg. Olivia was now clearly in Flavia's famous corner office, but somehow, the universe worked in her favor this time, as she could find a point of comfort on the horizon, across the Hudson: The most expensive *watch* in the world was visible on the other side of the river.

"Oliviaaaa! Welcome to *FW*." Flavia Wild's deep, low, confident tone broke the silence.

Olivia turned around to greet her.

"Flavia Wild." She then extended her hand to greet Olivia and continued with her signature British accent. "Lovely to meet you."

"Olivia Stone, and the pleasure is mine. "

"It's Olivia *Nicole* Stone, though, correct?"

"I've been told there's nothing you don't know." Olivia smiled and approved.

Flavia turned around toward a little tea table set up in the corner of the room and poured herself some without offering her crew any.

"David calls you Coco, though, right?"

"You must have friends on Wall Street," Olivia replied, then smiled, taking a sip from her water.

"Oh, darling, everywhere."

"My friends call me Vee also."

"Vee. Oh, see, now *that* I didn't know. VEE! I love it. Take a seat, Vee, and make yourself comfortable. We'll begin in a few minutes."

Olivia Nicole Stone "Vee" to friends, "Coco" to her husband and Wall Street – took a seat and gazed upon the most expensive watch in the world from across the river, and maybe for the first time in her life, she felt real and complete. Vee felt beautiful, Stone felt successful, Coco felt loved, Nicole felt at home, and Olivia could finally feel like the woman everybody around her saw. Perhaps today was the day she could let it all out.

The whole crew of photographers and sound technicians suddenly circled her like predators circle their prey, throwing all sorts of devices at her as part of the media and entertainment choreography – lights, cameras, microphones, and a touch of powder she really didn't want on her face. All signs they were about to begin.

"Allll right. Are we ready, people?" Flavia shouted at her team as she sat down on the chair in front of Olivia. She pulled up small cards with notes on the questions she had in store for Olivia and smiled at her: "I'm old school."

Olivia smiled back, took a deep breath, and took a final glance at the clock across the river as the assistant director started the countdown: *"3, 2, 1, rolling sound, speed, and we're live."*

"Olivia Stone, Hi!" A medium shot of Flavia Wild showed her on the director's little control screen, as she smiled at her guest in the most welcoming way.

"Flavia, it's an absolute pleasure." Olivia smiled back.

"Welcome, welcome, welcome to our Five for the Five for the Next Five series at *FW* magazine. You're one of the five women nominated this year, and what a year it has been for you, hasn't it?"

"That's right – quite the year."

"For those of you just hearing about Olivia Stone for the first time, buckle up. She's an icon in the advertising scene as one of the leading women to drive disruption. She's what some would call a veteran, though that always sounded very brutal to me, don't you think?"

"Well, the industry can be quite brutal," Olivia said, then smiled.

Flavia continued: "Olivia has won multiple accolades during her career, has mentored hundreds of young women looking for career direction, has added more than a dozen businesses to her agency's portfolio this year alone, and my question to her is just how does she do it? But you know, here at *FW* magazine, we talk business where it's none of our business…"

Flavia paused just enough to force a smile and acknowledgement from Olivia, then continued: "…and *especially* in the Five for the Next Five series, in which we cover the most successful stories of women leaders in New York. We want to know it all – what made you the Olivia Stone we all know, who supported you, who pushed you, what pulled you up to the high ground you're walking on today."

"I'll try to be an open book, Flavia."

"Wonderful. Just wonderful. So, first of all, it's Olivia *Nicole* Stone, isn't it?"

"Correct."

"So why is 'Nicole' such a secret?"

"It's not, but it's more of a family affair."

"It's the middle name only your parents know?" Flavia smiled.

"My parents used to call me Nicole. My grandmother's name was Nicole, and my mom lost her when she was still a teenager and wanted to honor her memory."

"How did that make you feel?"

"Never really thought about it, to be honest. I always felt loved in my house."

"You lost your parents years ago?"

"Yes, I lost mom to organ failure and dad to cancer."

"Tragic."

"It's always a tragedy when it happens to you. To the world, it's merely a statistic."

Flavia looked at her notes and moved on to the next card.

"Tell me about your childhood. What was it like? We read all these biographies lately from successful actors, singers, or athletes, and it seems like the spark to their engine was always a dad or mom who believed in them blindly and always pushed them to excel. I wonder whether it was the same in your home growing up."

"I think there's some truth to that. My parents were always very supportive of whatever I wanted to do; they never imposed anything on me."

"You come from middle class America?"

"Yes."

"I'm asking because, you know, on the flip side, there are other success stories about people who made it big starting from nowhere, having no support, no roof over their head, nothing. They comes from broken pasts and want to overcome their place in life."

"Yes."

"But that's not your story either?"

Olivia paused for just a split second, not because she didn't know how to answer, but because she wanted to give Flavia Wild the entertainment value she was looking for.

"No. I come from a regular middle class American family."

"I want to show a picture of you and your family when you were very young." Flavia turned toward the camera, showing a picture of her and her family on a yacht. "This is you, your dad, and your mom and their friends on a yacht in Miami. This doesn't really look like middle class to me."

"Life isn't made of a few years; it's made of decades. My parents had it all until they didn't."

"I sense there's more to the story here. I hope you don't mind, but Rick, my producer..." she then smiled and waved to this short guy with glasses sitting at the back of the room, "...he's a very curious specimen, so he did some digging on your family and found out that their company crashed way before the real estate crisis and never really recovered. How did that affect your life?"

"I was very young at that point; it's hard to understand at a young age. They always tried to provide as much as they could, and their story is probably no different than the story of many other families in America. Tragedy for me, statistics for others."

"How was your relationship with them?"

"I loved my mom very much. She was my best friend, so her death took a huge toll on me. My father and I never really had a relationship, to be honest."

"Why is that?"

"He was – absent. Never really got to know him well."

Flavia nodded, almost waiting for a continuation. If it was up to little Nicole, she would have hidden it, but this was Olivia Nicole Stone, and it had been a revealing year for her.

"He was an alcoholic." Olivia then smiled, knowing she gave her the answer she was waiting for.

"As the child of an alcoholic mother, I can tell you, I relate. I'm a statistic too. But to be fair, I actually think having an alcoholic parent history is now almost cliche."

"It was hard for me to talk about it for many years, and to be frank, it still is. My husband's family will be very surprised to hear this in your interview. "

"Why is that?"

"I'm nouveau riche, but let's just say this may be just a little too nouveau for them."

Flavia Wild laughed.

"Your husband – David Robertson – he was one of the hottest men in the New York City bar scene. I have three friends who would've given anything to go on a date with him, and now, if they open your Instagram account, it drives them nuts. You're the cutest couple ever."

"Thank you."

"I mean it. You two make it seem like you can really have it all. What's the secret?"

"Meeting in the middle."

"I think every woman in New York – and really the entire country – wants to hear how you can manage a successful career and a successful relationship. So how do you?"

"I have no idea." Olivia then smiled and made Flavia burst into laughter. "To be fair, we met in a moment in time when we both wanted a relationship, so we were available for one another. We both had very little time at hand and were ready to accept each other for who we are. It wasn't some crazy teenage infatuation. We always had respect for one another and always chased the same dreams."

"Did you have any big discords?"

Olivia paused again, but this time, Flavia wouldn't get what she was fishing for.

"No. Not more than any other couple has. The occasional fights over late hours or being late for dinner. We all just have to push through. Marriage is a job too."

"Hear, hear. What about kids?"

"Not yet."

"Why not?"

"It just hasn't happened yet."

"So, are you looking to have children?"

Olivia paused and looked at the clock.

"We don't know. We'll see if it happens."

"You know, I don't have kids. I was always afraid to given the career I've chosen for myself." Flavia Wild insisted on continuing with

239

this topic. "Do you think having children will make your career flatline?"

"Tough question. You know I think it depends on what kind of a fighter you are. If you're built to carry a young child with you on a plane for your meetings, if you can juggle through pitches and nannies, and still find serenity in the everyday, I don't think you'll flatline. But it's not easy. I don't think it's easy."

"Do you think companies should provide support for moms to be able to raise their children?"

"Oh, my opinion won't be the most popular, I'll tell you that. If we're striving for equality, I think we can't demand different advantages from men. We can't have a double standard."

"I can already see Twitter blowing up," Flavia Wild said with a smile, raising an eyebrow to Olivia's response. "You think David would accept splitting the chores with you if you had a baby?"

"No, I don't."

"Do you agree with that?"

"No, I don't." She smiled, "but the beauty of life is that we're all different with different personalities. We've somehow come to believe as a society that there's only one possible set of rules that we need to accept and that if anyone dares bend them, they shouldn't be worthy of our love."

"So, what would you do if you became pregnant tomorrow?"

"I'd have to tell you tomorrow."

"Are you pro-choice?"

"I hate labeling things. Each woman should do what she believes is right for her body and mind. I'm pro people not sticking their nose in what they shouldn't."

"I like that. So, advertising life. This is our first piece on women in advertising, and I must say I'm fascinated with your world. the ability to do something new every day, create content that can influence people, see your wildest imagination brought to life. But from the inside though, I hear that it's not all glitz and glamour, that after Wall Street, advertising is probably one of the most demanding after-hours jobs."

"Well, I don't know that that's entirely true, but it's definitely not for everybody."

"Which part is not true?"

Olivia smiled, as if it's obvious the answer is both, fueling a weird, tense, and estrogen-filled-room dynamic.

Flavia Wild continued: "You know, I read an article the other day about burnout in several fields and I always found it fascinating that even when a case of severe burnout comes out in the press, the stock for that company goes up on Nasdaq."

"Burnout seems like it's paying off then," Olivia acknowledged, smiling ironically.

Flavia Wild agreed: "And it's probably here to stay. How do you cope with burnout in your position?"

"I think in my position, I'm focused more on helping my teams not to burn out."

"But what about you? Shouldn't you put your mask on first to help yourself before you can save others?"

"My agency actually cares a lot about its leaders' mental well-being," Olivia reassured Flavia Wild, who listened skeptically, "but I think not all agencies do that. I think being a leader these days is harder than anything. They say it's really lonely at the top, but I think at the top, we're actually a group of depressed highly paid individuals who won't acknowledge each other's suffering and are in desperate need of an intervention. And every once in a while, we see one of us breaking – quitting the industry, taking decade-long sabbaticals, going the consultancy route. When we leave at this level, many times we close doors behind us, burn bridges, and don't look back so that we're never tempted to go back."

"What about your doors? Are they still wide open?"

"What do you mean?"

"I mean, do you still like what you're doing?"

"I love what I'm doing. To be fair, it's the only thing I know how to do."

"But do you still like where you're doing it?"

Olivia smiled and looked at Flavia Wild. She felt sweat coming through her blouse, reminding her that she made a decision and should stand tall.

"When is this show going to air?"

Flavia Wild lifted her eyes from her notes with curiosity. She knew she was about to get info that no one else had.

"In two weeks, but we're flexible," she replied.

"Then ask your question again."

"Are you still happy with being a leader in your current agency?"

"It's not a matter of happiness, it's a matter of choice. As of August 1, I chose a different path, and it'll be my last day with my current organization."

Flavia turned around to her producer, who was watching in disbelief.

"So, are you saying you're leaving?"

"That's correct."

"If you don't mind me asking – what's your next move?"

"I'll disclose that information in the coming months. I'm not at liberty now to do that."

Olivia answered, knowing that was a flagrant lie. She had no idea what she was about to do. Would she start her own business, freelance, or become a housewife against David's will? Who knew, but Olivia never felt and looked so certain about the decision she had made.

"Wow, well, good for you, Olivia. We're all rooting for you to see what you'll do next. As we're getting ready to say goodbye, I have a few questions that I'm asking every guest for this edition of Five for the Next Five."

"OK."

"If you could say something to Olivia Nicole Stone when she was 10 years old, what would you tell her?"

"That everything is going to be all right, that she's smart, beautiful, and that she can accomplish whatever she puts her mind to."

"What about Olivia Nicole Stone on her first day at her ad job?"

"Stand up for yourself, even if they call you a Stone."

Flavia Wild smiled.

"If you could look into the future, what would you tell your first kid?"

Olivia paused. Warmth surrounded her entire body, and for a split second, she felt like she was going to faint. Her blood pressure was definitely down, and she wasn't ready for this question.

"Olivia?"

"I would say I'm sorry."

Flavia paused. Somehow, she felt like she knew what was going on.

"Olivia, I know you always believed in living a life with no regrets. Do you have any?"

"I do. I have one, but I'll never be brave enough to talk about it." Olivia's eyes then flooded with tears.

"Turn off the camera. Do you need a minute?"

"No, I'm fine. Thank you."

"OK, last one. What would you say to someone just starting their career right now?"

"We are all born pure, then we become impostors. There's an impostor in all of us. Don't feel like you're doing something wrong, or that you're not right for the job. Believe in your abilities, work hard, and show yourself who you truly are."

END